CAPTAIN RANDOM

VS

THE SANDMAN

HAYDEN GRIBBLE

To Giulietta
Happy reading!
Hayden Gribble

ISBN 978-1-9998659-2-4

Printed and bound by Amazon

www.haydengribble.net

For Sophie

Also by this author

The Man In The Corner
Tales From Another Me
Child Out Of Time: Growing Up With Doctor Who In The Wilderness Years

PROLOGUE

A baron, desolated wilderness greeted the eyes of the travelers as their spaceship settled down on the sand dunes of the decimated world. The landing gear let out a whine - groaning under the stress and strain of hundreds of tons worth of titanium and seda metal that crunched the legs of the Venus II further into the ground, like a mallet hitting a tent peg into place.

Its battle worn colours and bleak, dense appearance blended in well with its surroundings on this occasion but given any other landscape and it would have attracted all the military and television crews of the galaxy to its whereabouts. In fact, given the huge exterior, that's what the Venus II normally did. But on this occasion, there was no fanfare. As the dust snaked and roared around the bottom of the ship, it began to settle on the stabilising pads that the Venus II stood on.

The only sound that could be heard now was the faint vibration of the inner door mechanism whirring away. All of a sudden, there a mighty hiss from the hydraulics and the door began to slowly drop down from the belly of the beast. Footsteps could also be heard clattering down the metal gangway. Well, if there was anybody around to hear it.

The shadows of three bodies illuminated the gangway - exposed by the bright, white lights from inside the spaceship. The first figure stood at the front of the pack and made his way heavily down the bottom of the ramp.

He bent down and touched the sand with his gloved fingers, feeling the coarse grains fall through the gaps between his digits. Sniffing, he shot a look back to his two companions. A young boy, who was no more than ten years old, stood on the ramp scratching his blonde hair, whilst observing the calm that surrounded them all.

The third member of the party, a girl of Earth-Indian descent, played nervously with her bag that swung irritatingly on her right shoulder. After several seconds of awkward silence, she decided to speak.

'So, we made it then?'

The first person looked away, knowing the answer but not wanting to dignify his friend with a response.

'Yes,' he croaked. 'Yes, we made it.'

'It's not what I expected,' cried the blonde haired boy.

He looked up at the strange fluorescent moon. Even though the moon was as bright as anything he had ever seen, the horizon still looked as dark as a harsh winter night back on Earth.

'I was expecting huge towers high in the sky and flying cars. What happened here?'

'The war to end all wars,' exclaimed the leader of the party as he straightened his legs and stood up. He could make out a faint outline of the once, great citadel in the far distance. 'Yet, it still rages. For centuries my home planet has been a battlefield. Millions upon millions have died and it was my responsibility to stop the fighting.'

The girl tore forward and put a reassuring hand on the shoulder of her companion.

'None of this is your fault, Random!' she insisted.

Random turned towards her and gave a glimmer of a smile from his dour expression. For all of the adventures both he and these two earth people had experienced, all the fun and laughs and the ever so slightly dangerous places they had visited in the quest to get back to this world, he knew he had made a terrible decision bringing them here.

'Anji, you will never know what suffering I have caused. It's time I made up for it.'

'How?' the boy asked.

'By making sure that this is the final day. I have to put it right, Jake. It is my destiny.'

Jake was worried. He had never seen Random so serious, so morose and so determined before.

Was this really the same boy that had whooped and cheered his way down a thousand foot rainbow on the planet Spectronia? Or the same spiky haired, funny costumed wearing guy who had used a discarded feather to tickle his way out of the prison tombs of Catacombe 62? Gulping hard, he took Anji's hands and followed his friend towards the unfriendly outline of what looked like a city.

Together, these three had been through so much. It had been the Earth children's choice to leave their planet behind and join this funny looking boy who fell from the stars and since they didn't have a home to go back to anyway, it didn't matter to them if they ever made it back. But at the same time, both Jake and Anji didn't want to get hurt. So far, they had endured many bumps and bruises on the planet hop back to Random's home world, but this time, there was a full scale war staring them in the face. And why had Random allowed himself to be talked into bringing them into the hornet's nest?

If I had a Dad, he'd never have let me come, Jake thought to himself as he trawled along the sand, which had entered a hole in his favourite pair of trainers and was causing more than a little irritation to his left foot.

'Back when we first met, I had no intention of letting you come with me,' Random said as he walked, the chilling night air carrying his sentence back into the general direction of his two friends. 'I just wanted to forget about my responsibilities, run away and never come back here. But you two, you two showed me how to be a better person and for that I thank you, but after we assess the situation and analyse what our next move should be I am taking you back to the Venus and locking the door. Do you understand?'

Jake and Anji nodded as they clambered through the soft sand.

'And what if you don't come back?' Anji's lips were beginning to feel sore as the wind continued to blow the sand in her face.

'Then Skateboard will pilot the ship to wherever you want and you can live your lives out however and wherever you like.'

'But you are coming back, aren't you?' Jake craned his neck to see if he could make out Random's face in the gloom.

Random felt terrible. Although he had the physiognomy of a boy just a couple of years older than his counterparts, he was in fact a far more advanced being than they were.

He was not as susceptible to illness, disease and trepidation like humans were but right now he had a throbbing feeling in his chest that he had never felt before. The most human of emotions.

Fear.

The trio jumped as Random's wrist communicator crackled into life. Over the wind, he could just make out a metallic voice.

'Sir, I must warn you that my sensors have picked up hostile lifeforms in your vicinity. It would be wise to come back to the ship as soon as possible.'

Random strained to be heard as he continued to walk.

'How many of them?'

'Fifteen, Sir. They appear to be on landhawkers, roughly 80 clicks away.'

'Okay, no problem. We are getting close to the edge of the citadel now. I will report back to you when we get there.'

The electronic voice was fast becoming less static than usual. You could almost say, it sounded emotional.

'Sir, I really must protest. Going on may result in your capture, or worse, deaths!'

'We have got the picture, Skateboard.'

'They will want to pluck all of your hairs out one by one whilst dancing the tango on your broken toes.'

'We get it-'

'...And they will dip you into a pit of boiling acid after making you wear dresses made of cat food so that their hammerhead tigers can have a bite at your-'

'SKATEBOARD...THAT IS ENOUGH!' Random bellowed. Jake and Anji jumped in fright. They had listened to every word. Maybe they should have stayed on the ship after all.

'Await my instructions,' Random ordered before clicking a switch on his communicator and returning to the task in hand.

'Would they really do that?' Jake enquired.

'Do what?'

'Make us wear dresses?'

Random sighed for so long it was heard by future generations. 'Come on, we are nearly there.'

The trio got down on their hands and knees as they negotiated the slight curve on the ground that licked up into the sky. 'Stupid bag!' Anji grunted as she swiped it over her shoulder, almost knocking Jake out in the process.

After a few minutes crawling in the dirt, they heard something they had not heard before. The wind had died down and all they could hear now was the sound of explosions, screams of pain and terror and the occasional whizz of hyperjet fighters and laser fire.

Random's heart was thumping so loud that he thought he could hear it over the sound of destruction.

'Right, that's it. Back to the Venus now, both of you!'

'We are not going anywhere,' Anji protested. 'We are staying by your side and that is final.'

'What? Are you mad!' Jake shouted. 'Can you not hear that down there!? Let's go while we still have the chance!'

'I'm staying.'

'Oh yeah? Well I'm going!'

The boys protests were interrupted by an explosion so loud it made the ground tremor for almost a minute.

'...On second thoughts, I'd better protect you, Anji!' Jake declared, despite cowering and holding onto the legs of his friend. She shot him an unimpressed glance.

'Stay low now, we have to get to the edge,' Random implored.

The three youngsters crawled their way closer and closer, the pitch black landscape was giving away to a blood red horizon, like a doomed sunrise. Slowly, they pulled themselves up to eye level and saw one of the most indescribable scenes of devastation it had ever been their misfortune to witness.

'Anji...Jake,' Random stuttered. 'This is the cidatel of the planet of Rodas. My home...'

CHAPTER ONE

ORIGINS

I

Every story needs a hero, a person who influences the lives of those around them in a positive way and generally saves the day. Somebody who wanders into town and rights the wrongs they see in front of them. Where there is danger, they make people safe. When the time of adversity comes, they hold their hand up to the storm and say, 'hey, you...stop!' Someone who will sacrifice themselves when there is no other option but to lay their life down to save many. Well, this story doesn't start with a hero. In fact, the word hero will not be used to describe our main protagonist until near the end. This is the story of… an idiot.

It started during the Galactic War of Ursa-17. A quadrant in the Galiony system, roughly 13 million miles away from the outer edge of our universe. The war had been raging since the system had first begun to shatter, like a window pane after a football is kicked through it. The proverbial football in this instance was an argument between the heads of two rulers of the planet known as Rodas.

It was a beautiful planet, where one side of the hemisphere was a crimson wash of red and the sun was a glorious yellow, irradiating the people with a warm orangey glow that kept them happy and blissfully unaware that they were being taxed heavily, that the international crime figures were high and that Paxley Dreamywonder, everyone's favourite celebrity reality television star on that side of the planet had been dead after tragically losing his life after a magazine coupon incident.

On the other side of Rodas there was a stark contrast. That side of the planet was a calming shade of electric blue and the sun looked more like a pinkish grey that bamboozled the people of that side of the hemisphere and had a habit of making them tired and irritable, especially when the moon was a florescent yellow that pierced even the blackest of black out paint. On this side, the people were not happy and were all too aware of the problems their world had inherited. Due to lack of sleep, the employed were forever falling asleep at work. There was next to no crime either, mostly because the criminals had a habit of only working at night and as the night time was lighter than the day, they simply didn't bother and just chatted to each other on webcams instead. Their Prime Minister had very little to lie about or cover up as there was simply nothing to keep secret. It should have been a happy place but it wasn't.

The frustrations of both factions soon came to a head when the rulers of the two sides, Cardinal

Beutoch of the red side and Cardinal Flavalboombuzzer of the blue, met for their annual senate meeting in The Grand Halfway Mountain on the equator of Rodas. It was a magnificent sight to behold. The mountain was a glorious amalgamation of all the colours of the known galaxies. Yellow, sepia, burnt orange, electric lime, screaming emerald, the colour formerly known as Prince and the one that was named after a man from the Wilburn'l system called Norman Astley.

There was however, one glaring omission from the canvas of colour and that was the one shade of light that neither had ever managed to create; that neither Parliaments had ever cracked or discovered, no matter how much of the public's money went unknowingly into its research. It seems silly now that this would seem such a humongous sticking point between the friendships of the good people of Rodas and the one thing that the people of the red and blue planet continued to fight about. They had never found a way of making the colour purple.

And so, for what seemed like the latest millennia of debates, Beutoch and Flavalboombuzzer sat wearily in their chairs at either end of the long, long delegation table. It was so long it stretched across international time zones and both leaders and their advisors had to speak through a combination of megaphones and intercom systems just to be heard. During this particularly tiresome session of deliberation, Flavalboombuzzer put down his goblet of hot milky tea right on his assistant's hand which was resting on the table and screamed his frustration down the megaphone so hard that it took the hair off the head of the scolded assistant.

'For god's sake, man!' he cried. 'Why will you not accept my advice and give it a go?' Flavalboombuzzer waited a full seven minutes for the reply.

'...What!?'

The elderly cardinal put his hand to his brow and wiped his golden fringe away to the side of his head.

'I said,' he sighed, 'why don't you just give it a go? Why won't sapphire and sodium work? It's the only combination we haven't tried!'

After a further seven minutes of waiting for his counterpart to respond, the intercom system fizzled into life.

'You mean YOU haven't tried! I've told you before how we have been conducting important experiments away from the public's view and not one of them worked.

When we did add sodium to the pure sapphire crystals in our possession, the explosion was so devastating that we had to cancel the month of

August and blame it on a change in the ecosystem,' Beutoch retorted. 'Our only action is to conduct our experiments in space out of harm's way so that we will not endanger the lives of our subjects.' He paused for a moment to read a set of notes handed to him by his personal assistant.

'Now let me see, what about white marzipan and wild watermelon? That should do the trick.' Flavelboombuzzer grunted in an impatient manner down the intercom. He exhaled deeply, emitting hot breath so loud that it reverberated around Beutoch's side of the table.

'Why do you think we sent that team of scientists up there?'

'To do that same experiment?' Beutoch enquired, his green skin perspiring in a way that made him look like a sunbathing lettuce.

'...To do that same experiment!' Flavalboombuzzer replied.

'And do you know what it did? Opened up a wormhole and dumped our scientists in a nude holiday resort on the other side of the galaxy!'

'Well...' Beutoch stalled. 'At least they were happy and safe on the other side.'

'They would have been if the nudist camp was not populated with deadly cyborgs who were giving their circuit boards an airing!'

Flavalboombuzzer screamed!

This debate went on for days. It rolled on for so long that Beutoch missed his 166th birthday party and Flavalboombuzzer missed his wedding anniversary, his divorce proceedings and finally his annulment.

Eventually, there could be no other way to settle this other than to declare full scale war on Rodas. It was news that plunged the whole planet into despair. The young men were recruited to join the armed forces. The children, who had been relatively happy in their well-funded and lovingly taught schools, were forced to attend work camps based on training them up to become the next generation of soldiers.

The elderly men and women were made to become nurses and medics where they were needed most.

The war raged long and hard and both Beutoch and Flavalboombuzzer both passed away during the early conflict.

Beutoch passed away from old age and his rival died after an unfortunate choking incident with an olive when his ship had to make a sudden emergency stop.

Soon, the other planets in the system also took the option of force to put an end to the bitter war. Some, like the Holy Planet of Xmir stayed unbiased and impartial to the events until someone pointed out that the very existence of religion in that part of the galaxy was based on war and conflict in the first place.

The fighting became so acrimonious that neighbouring planets struggled to keep out of the devastation. The Glogmeister Planet of Glop, where the inhabitants were sort of jelly like creatures who spoke out of the ear-shaped pods on the tops of their heads, were so afraid that they would also get caught up in the war that they moved planets to the outer system known only as 'for sale.'

Others so appalled at the reasons for the fighting, decided to hide the secret of the colour purple from the people of Rodas and also refused to take refugees in, saving them from the horror that ensued on their war-torn burning planet.

After two centuries of fighting, Rodas had become a bad word in an unforgiving galaxy, an outlawed fable, told to warn others off that part of space. The tales of Rodas were so bad that even the Hard as Nails Space bikers of Snotpoo 97 turned the other way when they were on the outer edge of Ursa-17.

If only someone had been smart enough to point out the obvious that red and blue make purple then many lives would have been saved.

But then again, our idiot would never have been brought into existence...

II

Blent stood with his arms crossed in the doorway, leaning against the cold marble. He stared unblinking into the main hall of the citadel of the blue side of Rodas.

It was night time, which of course meant it was the brightest time of the day for the occupants of that side of the planet and not the best time to have agreed to a secret meeting with a traitor. His pulse was racing like mad, scared that he would be caught and thrown into one of the many prison camps that had been built over what had seemed a lifetime ago. He had heard stories and they were not pretty ones.

His allies had created many unpleasant ways to torture those who had been captured. They were forced to take hour long baths with an animal called the Fargnot. The Fargnot looked like a mad scientist had managed to find a combination of a frog, a rabbit and a 17-tonne whale and it petrified the prisoners, especially as it would sing for six hours a day involuntarily and relentlessly.

The penalty for those who even attempted to escape was to ride the Fargnot around the camp with no clothes on whilst their fellow captors were made to fire hot lead at them from super soaker-like water pistols. Blent shuddered.

Who would want to suffer that kind of punishment?

He looked down at his watch. It was three in the morning. He had disappeared into the night and left his wife and child at home all alone. He had to get back soon, to protect them from the bombings and the attacks from the red side – who by now had called themselves the Crimson Empire. He lived just a few miles from the citadel, where the main bombardments happened. If all went to plan tonight, then the war would soon be over.

The old hall had so many memories for him; so many moments that would stay with him forever. This was where the people of the hemisphere had crowded upon the coronation of Queen Davinal around 900 years ago, long before the war had become a bleak, bloody mess that had no end in sight. As she took over her regional duties from her Father, there was an air of optimism and excitement that filled the sapphire side of Rodas. A promise was made that day; that the war would be over by the end of the year.

Sadly, after Her Majesty's mysterious disappearance, there was nothing but never ending chaos and bloodshed.

It was the last time that Rodas had dared to dream of a new world as the current one plunged further into chaos.

Blent's train of thought was disturbed by the sound of distant footsteps. He jolted, his eyes darting like mad from side to side, looking in desperation for a place to hide. There were none. The citadel was nothing but smooth spherical shapes, cobbled together by a designer who thought that straight edges were just as dated as flared jeans are on planet Earth. A sense of panic began to grip Blent, who pulled the collar of his long, dark trench coat up to his face and then tip-toed across to a half-mooned crevis that would fit his seven-foot-tall frame. It was at moments like this that he wished he hadn't inherited his uncle's ridiculously lanky frame. He thought to himself that he probably looked like a large worm cowering behind a small crisp.

The footsteps were getting louder and louder until all of a sudden they stopped. Blent dared himself to sneak a peek from his not-so-hidden hidey hole.
He slowly reared his head up and over the crevis, which still would have given a lot away as his head was almost as long as his body. His forehead was so large that a family of hedgehogs could happily call it their holiday home. Nevertheless, he just had to see who it was who was making his...or her...way into the citadel.

For a few moments, there was nothing but silence. It was the most unnerving experience of Blent's life so far. He was just one sneeze, one cough away from a naked ride on a Fargnot.

Sweating profusely, he strained his vision to see the outline of a lone, dark shadow, sprawling out long onto the citadel floor.

'Hello? Is anybody there?'

Blent sighed so hard he nearly sucked his lungs up into his throat. He strode out like a different man from behind his hiding place, confident and assured. The sound of a woman's voice, soft and as beautiful as a nightingale in the moonlight beckoned him closer.

'Thank god it is you. I thought I was a goner for a minute there!'. As Blent walked closer towards the shadow, he saw the figure of a much smaller person come into view.

'I'm sorry I'm so late. It's a nightmare to get past the soldiers at this time of night. Also, I may have got a little bit lost. I've never been to this side of Rodas before.'

Blent looked upon the face of his ally. It fitted the voice perfectly. Strong, assured, intelligent, determined, beautiful. Whilst studying her face, he also noticed something he had never seen before about her. Her face was a crimson red. Crimson Empire Red.

'It's a good thing I recognised your voice,' he said. 'The only people I have seen with that shade on their skin have either been after my blood or imprisoned in the camps.'

His female companion shook her head. 'Is that what this planet has come to? Torn apart by colour? Lesser planets have learned to resolve their petty discriminations. It is a disgrace that ours never has.'

'If all goes to plan tonight, Niva...it will.'

Blent held his arm out, beckoning Niva to walk with him.

'Come, there is little time.'

The pair walked down the long, white corridor of the citadel at a pace that would make the average person gasp for air after a few hundred feet.

There was no time for small pleasantries or catching up. They were lucky to have got as far as they had.

It had all started when Blent, sitting alone in his laboratory, intercepted a message on his mailing list.

He had long given up the desire to end the war by discovering the colour purple and after a number of decades had decided to cease his experiments, making him the latest in a long line of Government-enlisted academics who had attempted to crack the case and failed.

Instead, seeing how bad things had got and worrying for the safety of his family, he decided to secretly research the underground revolutionaries who had begun to fight for peace. He had heard rumours that the revolution groups were a mix of people from both sides of the planet.

At last, unity! And not just that, but these people were peaceful. He was entranced at how they worked towards a better future. All those meetings, all those sing-a-long's about ending the war. All those bonfire evenings under the crust of Rodas, hidden away from view like moles, and like moles, they were slowly digging up to the surface.

As the revolutionaries grew in number and Blent became more and more involved in the peace efforts, the revolution was taking measures to infiltrate the main army bases on both sides and sabotaging them from within.

There were many people like him who had also been employed by the Government, so access was easy. They all went by codenames to protect their identities and went about trying to bring down the establishment from within.

But slowly, the armed forces had worked out what was happening and had started to clamp down on the revolutionaries.

Blent had been lucky not to have been found out so far. He knew this was his last chance. He had been put in contact with a mysterious woman called Niva through one of the remaining revolutionaries. The numbers had dwindled as those who were discovered had been imprisoned in camps and punished severely. So to maintain secrecy, neither of them had seen each other's face. They had only contacted through instant mailing and scrambled telephone conversations. This was their first proper meeting and if they failed, then they both knew that they would never see their loved ones again.

Niva looked to her right and saw the pensive look on Blent's face. Like he, she had been driven to desperate measures to ensure that the Rodasians had any future at all. She was from a more military background than her co-conspirator.

She had been enlisted as a young child to become a pilot in the Sedlich Infantry and aged just 15 she was flying her way into warzones, taking out the enemy and using her armed combat skills to take prisoners who had dared infiltrate the red side of the planet. But after years of fighting, her resolve was destroyed when the Crimson Empire decided to dye the armies' skin a permanent red colour as a reminder of who they fought for and where they came from. Like so many others, Niva knew that this was wrong and that it would inspire more hate from their opponents. This war had gone too far. Her innocence and youth had been taken by the conflict, and now so had her identity.

Luckily, Niva was discharged from the army after she faked her own death on the day of the bloodiest battle the war had ever seen. The day of the Emergence.

III

'Are you sure this is going to work? Niva said without looking at her partner in crime. 'This kind of thing has never been tried before.'

Blent stared at her, as if she had just told him that she thought he could not spell. Or count.

'Of course it will work!' he snapped. 'I have been working on the formula for the last five years. It hasn't been tried and tested, granted, but I know this is the answer to all of Rodas' problems.'

Niva sighed. She had second thoughts. It was an ambitious project and she had more confidence in a man surviving a fall from a thousand feet into a cushioned yoghurt pot than what they were attempting. 'But how did you come up with it?'

Blent gave a moment's pause to draw breath. It was a long story.

'Back when I was project leader on the Nirmamas Outposting Scheme, I attended a conference about how the discovery of the only colour to be missing from the spectrum could be sliced from the memories of species from the outer reaches of our galaxy.

Since the peoples of the universe had turned their backs on Rodas long ago, the chair of the conference, Professor Travemant, had started experimenting on prisoners of war; extracting memories, skills and abilities from them to be implanted in soldiers who were lacking all of the above and turn them into a kind of super-warrior.'

'And that's what you're going to do here? Simply make another warrior? I don't suppose it may have escaped your attention but we have enough of them as it is! In fact you could say that the vast quantity of soldiers in this world has led to centuries of war!' Niva spat. She was so angry that she had left the red hemisphere to risk her life just to make another killer. 'There has been enough bloodshed. One more soldier is just another drop in the polluted ocean.'

Blent stopped in his tracks. He looked hurt, his eyes squinting to see through Niva's perspective. He looked down at her, eclipsing her like the moon shutting out the sun.

'I'm not going to add to all of the death and destruction, Niva...I'm going to create a miracle. For you, for me, for Rodas, for the rest of this stupid, idiotic galaxy. I'm going to create life.'

The lanky scientist continued down the long, white corridor, leaving Niva to stand on the spot for a moment.

'Oh, my god,' she thought to herself. 'He's flipped!'

She looked ahead and saw that Blent had sprinted away from her. Breathing in, she ran off after him. The clock was ticking...

*

Meanwhile, high above the citadel, a heli-fighter continued its patrol of the burning capital. Inside the dark, cramped, hawk-shaped machine were two soldiers, both dressed in black leather combat suits, which kept their bodies thin and nimble but compressed their flabby, middle-aged frames into that reminiscent of a body builder.

The Pilot had set the steering console to automatic control, so that he and his counterpart, a young, stick-thin boy fresh from the academy, could watch the intergalactic football match between Gloicchester United and the Steaming Vom Wiglacers of Nubulus 3.

As they squinted to see who had possession of the ball, which was spherical but with metal spikes in it as to make for a harder game, it was clear that the pair had neglected their duties.

Instead of being on watch for intruders inside the citadel and warding off any unwanted spies from the Crimson Empire intent on bombing what was left of the capital, they were arguing over who was the better side, even though the Steaming Vom Wiglacers of Nubulus 3 were currently edging the tie 45-3.

'I'm telling you son,' the Pilot garbled to his young ward through a homemade turkey sandwich. 'Gloicchester will never stand a chance if they insist on playing without a goalkeeper.'

The youngster squinted away, trying to make out the players on the pitch through a haze of bad reception that had turned them into static, explosions of colour on the relatively small television screen.

'True. But perhaps they would if your side didn't have thirty-nine players on the pitch! I thought intergalactic football was a five-a-side affair?'

The Pilot gulped the remnants of his lunch down. 'Ah, you'd have thought. But you know what that business is like. Offer the referee a bribe or two and the pitch is your oyster!'

He itched his torso with some discomfort. These suits were incredibly stuffy and suffocating. After a while, they became like a second skin.

The suits had been constructed to give a more dynamic and professional feel to the armies of the blue hemisphere.

What they disguised underneath - for the majority of the armed forces - was middle aged spread. The problem was that these suits were designed with a special compression containment field on the inner lining so it kept the illusion on the outside. They were impossible to take off. You had to spend all day in them. Eat in them, sleep in them, bathe in them. Going to the toilet was only possible with the installation of special zips at the front and bottom of the wearer and even that mostly proved tricky...and messy.

Now that the army was old and knackered and had no idea how unfit it was thanks to the ignorance installed by the miracle suits, some of them had started to breakdown. Little tears in the fabric had begun to emerge and the inner fibre had started to make the wearers itch and scratch. There were dark, grizzly stories being told about what happened to the men as their suits tore apart. It didn't make for easy bedtime reading. But the duo were ignorant of what was in store. As the Pilot continued to claw at the patch on his stomach, something he had been doing for some time, he ran his fingers over his taut six pack.

'I never thought I'd live to 57 and still have a body like this,' he said. 'Still, it must be all the fighting we have been doing. Keeps you fit, son, keeps you fit.'

'But you told me the other day that you haven't seen combat in twenty years,' the ward pondered. 'You told me that your regiment had been attacked and you lost the function of your legs.'

'Well,' the pilot rolled his bottom lip. 'I may of told a fib here and there.'

'Indeed. I knew you were lying because you've walked ever since I got posted here three months ago!'

'Too late to dob me in now, lad. Who would you go to? My superior officer is dead.'

'I know,' the ward replied. 'You killed him!'

'It was a mercy killing.'

'He was on holiday! You managed to fix a timed explosive to the alarm clock of his holiday villa. I'm sure you would have got away with it if you hadn't tweeted the whole thing was your doing.'

The Pilot grimaced. He was pleased that social media has since been banned on all planets within Ursa-17.

'It's amazing what comes out when you've had a few too many ginger ales.'

The Pilot leant forward to pick up his beverage of choice; a ginger ale. Not that he had spotted it, but a tear had begun to form in the area of his suit that he had been scratching.

'That's why I was given this post. Call it exile it you like. Whatever you call it I'm afraid you're stuck with me.' He took a look at his counterpart. The leather suit was so large it looked like he was a little boy wearing his dad's wedding jacket. Pathetic, he thought to himself. 'Why hasn't your suit started to fit your frame lad?'

The ward looked down. His long, dark hair dangled over his face, hiding his pale, white features from view as he glanced at his puny body.

'I don't know,' he replied. 'Maybe mine had a defect.'

'You won't last long in front of a hail of bullets if your suit isn't doing its job!' The Pilot took a swig of his ginger ale and leant back in his chair. As he did, the tear got a little larger in length.

The heli-fighter lurched in the sky as it continued its pre-planned sweep of the city. Little did it know what place it had in the creation of the potential saviour of Rodas.

The ward looked up and saw the pile of leftovers shoved into the corner of the small craft. It was hideous how much the Pilot was eating.

'Maybe if you shared the grub, I would fill it out!'

The Pilot grunted like a warthog struggling to fit into a summer dress.

Ignoring the fact that he did overeat, and had done for decades, he replied, 'What with the measly rations we are given? Huh? You stick to what you're given mate!'

The ward sat slumped in his chair and looked at the altitude dial. It was ever-so-slowly decreasing. He furrowed his brow, perplexed as to why this could be.

'Sir.'

'Not now, young lad. Gloicchester have just pulled a goal back. This could get tight, this match! It's 45-4 now!'

The Pilot heard a squelching noise emit from inside his suit. He thought little of it, but then he felt a constricting sensation in his left leg.

'Then again, it's not the only thing that is getting tighter...'

What happened next filled the young ward with terror. Right in front of his eyes, he witnessed the pilot change. At first, there was the sound of tearing fabric. The suit began to rip without mercy. The Pilot's face was awash with horror and fear. He started sweating, his face became hot with anxiety and his eyes grew evermore bloodshot.

'It's the compression containment field...it's breaking down!' he screamed as he got up off his chair.

His left leg began to feel swollen and painful like an army of hornets had stung it mercilessly. Soon, the feeling spread up his body, into his torso, which began to bulge against even more tears in his suit. The Ward reached the intercom system.

'Zeta Major, this is Black Hawk we have a problem here.'

The intercom sparked instantly into life. A computerised voice replied through the metal grill of the speaker.

'Roger that Black Hawk, what is the situation?'

'The Pilot...' the ward broke off as he watched his superior continue to swell in random parts of his body. He was starting to develop thick rolls of fat under his chin and his limbs were now out of proportion with his body. His arms were so flabby he was having trouble lifting them as the suit continued to tear apart.

'...his suit has broken down. He is getting bigger and bigger, Sir, what do I do?' The panic in the ward's voice was reaching fever pitch.

The intercom went dead. The youngster struggled to make anything out over the screams of the Pilot, who was getting very large by now.

A balloon-like, pinkish belly was poking out of the hole in the torso of his suit. It looked like he was going to blow.

The ward looked at the heli-fighters instruments. They were still losing height. He was panicking so much now that his right hand that was resting on the console had started to shake. All of a sudden, the intercom came to life again.

'I have spoken to my superior and he has asked me to relay this message...FOR GOD SAKE, GET OUT OF THERE MAN!'

The loud volume of the latter half of the message made the ward jump. He was so frightened he had been frozen on the spot. He daren't look at the Pilot, who by now had grown so fat and big that he had crushed the TV against the pile of rubbish in the corner. He looked terrible. Like a man who had been blown up by a foot pump.

The heli-fighter began to spin uncontrollably. It scraped the main tower of the citadel with its propeller as the ward, who had been forced to snap himself out of the shock of what was happening, tried to wrestle some control back from the craft.

'It's no good, lad. Save yourself!'

The Pilot yelled. His voice sounded wheezy and strained, as though his vocal cords were now swimming in the fatty deposits exploding all over his swollen body.

The first tear in the Pilot's torso shredded across his jelly-like skin and he screamed as he continued to get bigger. He was now six times the size of a normal person. The compression containment field had gone haywire and was now stretching him to breaking point, pulling him apart.

'Shut the door lad! You won't want to see this!' he demanded.

The ward did just that, knowing there was nothing he could do to save the pilot. He flicked a switch on the console and the door slid shut. All he could hear was the screams and the failing engines. The heli-fighter was getting closer and closer to the ground. The ward realised that he had blocked himself off from the only exit he could have used to escape.

He knew that when the craft went down, it would probably mean the end of him too. For a few ghastly seconds, he let that horrific thought wash over him like a wave of death. Then suddenly, he heard a final terrible yelp from the pilot before it got much worse.

A massive explosion ripped through the craft, sending the ward crashing up against the console and then up against the viewing window.
The sound was deafening. Flames omitted from the outer shell of the heli-fighter as the explosion hit the fuel tanks and the ammunition that was stored directly below the section that the pilot had been in. The fire spread along the small craft but stayed out of the control room as the ward regained his seating position.

He grappled with his senses and ignored the pool of blood that was running down his face from a fresh gash in his forehead. He tried to pull the craft up but it was no use. The heli-fighter was about to crash into the citadel...right where Blent and Niva were about to formulate their plan...

IV

Blent and Niva were agonisingly close to the laboratory, blissfully unaware of the madness that was ensuing high above them. Niva was blowing hard, doing her best to keep up with her impressively tall counterpart.

Her cheeks were puffed out and she made an effort of conserving a gulp of breath for a few moments before exhaling loudly from her screaming lungs. She was having a rough time keeping up with Blent but then that was to be expected.

After all, watching him sprint further and further away made him look like a daddy longlegs trapped in a bathtub. She would have giggled if he wasn't so damn fast and their mission was so grave.

'Come on!'

The scientist had decided that they needed to run to get to the safety of his laboratory as he had grown anxious about the possibility of them being discovered and failing in their mission.

He clutched his inside pocket with his right hand.

Inside, Niva had given him the essential ingredients to his experiment and he would do anything to make sure that they were not damaged.

A thought crossed his mind as he was just a few metres away from the door. He held on his person the only thing that could save Rodas.

Blent finally made it to the smooth, silver coloured door that opened up onto what had been his working space for the last few years. He tried to turn the handle but it failed to budge.

'Oh, of course!' he muttered. 'Silly me. Don't worry Niva; thank god I remembered the key.'

'Yeah, like you're going to leave a laboratory full of top secret files and research open in a war zone,' Niva screamed at her companion. Her reply echoed down the corridor. Blent sighed. She was miles away. Still, it gave him a little time to dig the long, serrated key out of his pocket. He dug deep into the murky depths of the multitude of pockets on his coat. First, he checked his left-hand-pocket. Nothing but an old tissue and a green, disappointed looking chocolate sweet in the shape of a ques-bear he had taken from home a month ago but had forgotten to eat.

He quickly searched the other pocket. There was what felt like a card that had got stuck to the frayed inner stitching, which was clinging onto the card like its life depended on it.

He pulled and pulled until he heard a huge tearing sound that echoed through the dark, long corridor.

Wincing as though he had just dropped some expensive china on a glass floor, Blent looked inside the envelope and gazed at the front of the card. The words 'Happy Anniversary' were emblazoned in pink and red font on the front. Blent sighed. He had been so preoccupied he had forgotten to open the card. He grunted when he realised that his anniversary was a couple of days ago. *If we make it out of this alive,* he thought, *it will take more than a card and a peck on the cheek to keep her in my life.*

Shaking his domestic problems from his thoughts, Blent reached inside his inner pocket to put the card away. As he did, his long, snakelike fingers clumsily knocked Niva's secret leather pouch from its relative safety. Blent gasped and for a few seconds his life seemed to be running in slow motion. His eyes grew wild with horror as he bent down to the ground to catch the pouch but he expected he would not make it in time.

If the components in the pouch broke on impact on the cold, marble floor then that was it.

All of his hard work, all of the jeopardy and danger he had faced with the revolutionaries had led to this moment and now it was about to go up in smoke.

Out of the corner of his right eye, he saw a hand dive out towards him, reaching out low to the ground.

His eyes followed the pouch as it dropped softly into the palm of the outstretched hand. Blent breathed a sigh of relief.

'What do you do for an encore?' she inquired. 'Stand in front of a nuclear blast!?'

'Sorry, Niva. I'm just nervous. I'm not normally this clumsy.'

As the word 'clumsy' left his lips, Blent's hand slipped on the floor as he tried to get up and he whacked his chin hard on the ground. Niva rolled her eyes before offering her other hand to her fallen comrade. She bent down and helped him up.

The red-faced girl took the key from Blent and jammed it hard in the lock. She manipulated it; turning it left and right until she heard the lock click open. She pushed the heavy door and spilled inside the laboratory, pulling the still-startled Blent inside. With a great effort, Niva pushed the door closed behind them, allowed herself a sigh of relief and looked at her comrade. What now?

'We'd best leave the lights off. There is a glass ceiling above us. Wouldn't want to light ourselves up like a star going supernova now would we?'

Blent started to fumble around on the harsh stone floor. Niva looked at her surroundings. The laboratory was a pig sty.

Piles and piles of paper covered the work benches, glass beakers we left all over the floor and there seemed to be a chalkboard that had overturned and fallen flat on another desk that was now smothered by shattered glass. Niva took a peek at what had broken the fall of the dilapidated board. It looked like a cage of some sort - transparent and hard – at least it had been. Just as Niva bent down to take a closer look, a strong, repugnant and sickening smell surged down her nostrils and made a nest in the back of her throat. Suddenly she leaped back. Something had been alive in that cage when the chalkboard slipped off its buckled haunches and obliterated it. From the smell, it definitely wasn't alive now.

'Remind me never to ask you to pet sit for me!'

Blent ignored the remark and was already busy pulling a large piece of tarpaulin off a machine in the centre of the room. Niva gazed at the monstrosity that eclipsed her thoughts for the poor deceased lab pet.

The machine was roughly twenty feet in height, thin and silver and stood like a tower in the dark.

'How long did it take you to make this?' she asked.

'Oh not long. As soon as I had run a few tests and realised that it was possible to fabricate new life from Professor Travement's original notes, I just knew that this would be our salvation.'

'How does it work?'

'Well, imagine that this is a food blender…'

Niva huffed. 'Right…not the best visual comparison Blent.'

'Just imagine that it can mix up all of the ingredients of a cake, or a smoothie, take your pick! Then it filters out the pips and leaves us with a completely invincible, physically tough, devastatingly intelligent…'

'Smoothie?' Niva interrupted. 'Okay I get it, just press the start button already. I have a feeling that something bad is about to happen.'

'Will you relax?' Blent looked at her with calm, reassuring eyes. 'Nobody can get to us now. We are just one step away from completing our mission and then…Rodas will be saved.'

'Well if you're sure…'

'Look, I'll let you stand guard at the door if needs be.'

Blent turned towards the machine and flicked a switch on the crude keypad which looked like it had been added to the cylinder as an afterthought.

He jabbed a few buttons and a compartment popped open. Inside were several vacant file holders with what looked like the lip of another cylinder on top.

This was where the liquid from within the tubes was going to be sucked up into the machine and life would be created.

Niva crossed her arms, gazed up through the glass roof and sighed. Her attention then went back to the cylinder, which was beginning to hum into life. Blent furiously managed the controls like a madman playing a reaction game and she braced herself for the worst.

'There we go…now we wait. It shouldn't take long. Give it a few minutes to sift through the information and then we shall have our miracle!'

Blent's optimism would be crushed in a little over four minutes. Unknown to the duo, their plans were about to unravel quicker than a ball of wool tumbling down an endless flight of stairs.

Just moments before the process was complete and the proclaimed saviour of Rodas was fully formed, ready to end the bitterness that had engulfed the once-mighty planet, the glass ceiling splintered into a thousand pieces, showering down like razors on the unsuspecting freedom fighters.

A heli-fighter plummeted through, crashing to the laboratory floor in a dust cloud of smoke and fire.

Blent and Niva reeled back as the force of the crash hurled them against the wall, knocking the former unconscious and the sonic boom of the blast permanently damaging Niva's hearing for the rest of her life. After what seemed like an eternity, the perished heli-fighter came to rest on the floor and the laboratory decimated beyond all recognition.

Slowly, Niva stirred and picked herself up. The first thing she noticed was that there was an insistent ringing in her ears that hadn't been there before. It was overpowering and frightening that nothing else was audible. She gazed around the room in horror. She could imagine the sound of the flames licking maniacally around what looked like a crashed Crimson Empire heli-fighter. There was no point checking for survivors, she thought to herself. No-one could have survived such a hideous accident. Her attention then turned immediately to Blent.

She recoiled in devastation as she saw that her ally, the man who had given hope to the people of Rodas, lay lifeless on the ground; his head slumped against the wall.

A trickle of blue blood had smeared down the wall from the point of impact. She looked at the lifeless form and noticed what looked like a card poking out of his lab coat.

Forlorn, Niva swooped for the card, knowing that it had some sentimental value to the scientist but not knowing the reason why. She knelt down to check for a pulse in vain hope but it was no use. Blent was dead.

Suddenly, the scientist's machine started to yawn with greater ferocity than before and the whole cubicle started to shimmer. In all the turmoil, Niva had forgotten about her mission objective. It was a miracle that the damned contraption hadn't been damaged in the accident! She staggered over the broken glass and twisted metal to the impossible contraption. Niva peered inside the class container and noticed a humanoid body suddenly whirring into form, as the fog cloud within slowly began to combobulate.

Niva started to feel dizzy; an effect from the smoke emitting from the crashed heli-fighter. She gasped as she realised that the craft ran on methane and bromide fuel and when unleashed with oxygen, the effects were toxic. Niva started to pant heavily, sweat forming on her brow as it dawned on her that she didn't have much time left…

She clasped her hands up against the glass as the humanoid's form became solid, the seconds ticking away before its 'birth.'

The machine shook more violently than before and as Niva began to slip slowly down the shaft, her life force leaving her body, the hum from the cubicle grew louder and louder and LOUDER! Until…

DING!

The sound of an egg timer signaled the end of the birth…and the beginning of life. The chamber door creaked open and clouds of smoke spilled out like a milky tide of fog into the decimated laboratory. Niva blinked upwards from her vantage point on the ground, gasping for air. In her final moments she saw the large shadow of a man loom over her, engulfing her frame. Her lungs began to burn. Gulping and fearing that this was the end, she struggled with all her might to stay alive long enough to set her eyes on the man that she had helped create.

Sadly, her final breaths were accompanied with a feeling of failure and utter humiliation. As the figure in the chamber stepped forward, his shadow diminished in height to a little over five feet tall. She shook her head as her bloodshot eyes screamed out in agony.
'Bloody…scientists!' she hissed to herself as her head collapsed to the ground.

What Niva and Blent had struggled to create, all those man hours, dangerous meetings and life-threatening missions they had both taken part in, had led to nothing. For in the chamber door, stood - not the man who would put an end to the bitter war on Rodas - but the body of a young boy…

V

The boy staggered out of his cocoon and into a world of chaos. Opening his new-born eyes for the first time, he saw nothing but devastation, death, broken glass and twisted metal. He blinked through the smoke which brought tears to his eyes like a freshly cut onion. He cried out in shock as he noticed the dead form of Niva at his feet. Scrambling away from the corpse, he then noticed another dead body in the corner of the room and shivered. Although he was just moments old, he was already well aware of the finality of death. He was surrounded by it!

His mind and thoughts darted all over the room. The fireball in the middle of the laboratory, the two corpses, the turmoil; it was all too much for a new being like him and before he knew it, the boy was running.

He had no idea where, but his naked legs were carrying him as far away as he could, away from the horror that was now scarred into his memory.

As he pelted like a thunderbolt down the cold, dark corridors of the citadel, he heard a voice in his head that was telling him his purpose - what he was supposed to do.

It was too much to take in. Save a planet!? He

wasn't even wearing any clothes! And why should that responsibility rest on his pre-pubescent shoulders? Why not that of a great general, a battle scarred hero? The questions continued to rain down upon him. Who was the lanky, blue man in the incredibly white coat and the red skinned girl who both lay dead by his feet? Were they his parents?

He didn't even have time to look down and observe his own form – he didn't care how he looked. He just wanted to escape and get out of there.

*

'Sergeant, they came down in what looked like the medical centre on the west wing of the citadel.'

The crash of the heli-fighter had not gone unnoticed by those conflicting factions over the sky of the citadel – not to mention those in the tactical war room back at the Crimson Empire's base. The call taker sat feverishly typing the developments into his log book.

Sergeant Everald stood gazing out of the observatory window, taking in the view and pondering his next move.

The Tactical Ensign had informed him minutes earlier that the pilot's suit had malfunctioned and the chaos that had ensued had caused the accident. His crossed arms dropped to his side and he marched over to the operator's station.

'Send a recovery team in to retrieve the black box. No-one outside of this room will find out about what happened. We don't want the enemy to know our suits are degrading. There's no way that I am giving them the upper hand and I certainly don't want members of the boardroom getting word of our weakness.'

The operator felt a sharp sensation swipe across his cheek…well one of the four cheeks on his face he had at his disposal. He felt his hot, aching face and looked in fear into the eyes of his superior.

'I will not hear that word in my presence!' Everald spat. Regaining his composure, his voice returned to its cool calm tone.

'Can we hack into the citadel's security system? I want to know what happened as soon as possible.'

The operator gulped and turned back to his work.

His fingers flickered against the keys in quicksilver fashion and although he was doing his best, he could hear the tap-tap of the Sergeant's boot clanging impatiently on the metal gantry floor. Mercifully, he managed to infiltrate the security system after bypassing the firewall mainframe - which was practically a room with computers in that ran the security systems in the citadel and could not be reached as there was a wall in flames in the hacker's way.

'All done, Sir,' he declared.

Together, Everald and the operator saw it all; Blent and Niva, the genesis machine, the crash of the heli-fighter and eventually the unnatural creation of a brand new being in the glass chamber.

With intent, Everald lent closer into the viewer screen.

'Show it. Show it on the ultra-screen!' Everald barked.

The operator pressed a few buttons and transferred the images onto the giant 50 foot awning that dominated the room. Every man and woman stopped precisely what they were doing. From the military to the pen pushers, every single person paused in their steps and gazed in shock and awe at the fantastic sight.

Even the secretary who was making the Sergeant his late-night coffee had her sight fixed on the images and found herself pouring the muddy liquid all over the floor instead of his mug.

'I don't believe it,' Everald gasped. 'Get a search party down there, now...NOW, gadzuke it!'

The operator turned back to his post and radioed in to the foot soldiers.

'All units…I repeat, all units. Engage the citadel. I repeat. Engage the citadel!'

Everald gazed up at the image. Something he had never seen before, so brilliant yet devastating he was struggling to work out what to do next. In front of him, projected for all to see, was a boy…with purple skin…

*

The newborn continued to race through the citadel, totally oblivious of the chaos his very existence was about to cause.

His legs carried him at such a vast speed that the broken glass and masonry that littered the floor pinged off his naked soles like bullets against a wall of steel.

He had no idea where he was running, but an overwhelming sense of fear and desperation led him to flee anywhere. His mind was still empty, except for two voices that kept crawling over his thoughts.

'You are the only person to save us all,' said one of the ghostly apparitions.

It was the voice of a woman, whilst the other was that of a man and it was encouraging him to, 'be the bridge between a world that is divided.'

He didn't even know what a bridge was!

Choking as the air was replaced by the poisonous concoction of poison and fire, the boy tore through a wooden door into the open hallway of the citadel. The place was amber with flame, with one half of the outer wall ripped open. Skidding to a halt, the boy caught his breath and surveyed his surroundings. A cold wind chilled through his cloth-less form and he shivered as he looked for an escape route. Before he could take in another breath, a crash of sound broke above him and a halogen light that burnt deep into his newly formed retinas pushed the boy to the floor. Shielding his vision with his arm, he tried in vain to protect his ears from the piercing scream of engines above him.

'Alright, now we don't know who you are or what you are, but you've got to come with us, kid.'

The boy looked away, confused and alone. The voice came from the whirring contraption above him and sounded like it was coming through some form of amplifying contraption.

'Stay where you are and we will come in and get you.'

The voice spoke with the utmost authority as it buzzed through the cold night air. The boy began to convulse, his body in shock at its first few moments. Tears began to form in the corners of his eyes and no matter how hard he tried to blink them away, they showed no signs of stopping. Resigned to his fate, he curled into a ball and wept.

'Iron Hand, Iron Hand, this is...erm…the Sacrificial Lamb here.' The young Private shook his head at the indignity of his call sign. He could not wait until he was no longer the new boy in the squadron so that he could relinquish the agonizing title. 'We have found the child, Sir. We will proceed with the pick-up and report back when the mission is accomplished.'

Everald stood incandescent with his arms fixed like tent poles over the intercom system. 'Don't just stand there, man!' he barked into the microphone. 'For flibs sake, get on with it!'

'Yes, Sir…'

The Privates reply was cut out by a savage blow to the speaker, delivered from the impatient hand of the raging Sergeant. The speaker hissed and a puff of smoke emitted from its mangled mesh as the whole room stopped in fear.

They had seen the Sergeant like this before - and when his anger reached fever pitch like this, it always meant that the next couple of hours were going to be the most crucial in the Crimson

Empire's cause and that the control crew's desk was going to need to be fixed again for the fourth time that month!

Without a moment's hesitation, Everald wheeled on his heels and marched smartly into his office in the corner of the main operations bay. He pushed his palm against the print recognition screen and the door sliced into the wall allowing him entry. Stomping to his desk, he poured over the list of buttons that accompanied his own personal intercom.

Much like its wounded counterpart, it too was dented and mangled from many an encounter with the iron fist of the cantankerous Sergeant.

As if like a sentient being, it almost squirmed in its place as Everald punched the big red button at the top of the list.

He waited for the buzz to whimper into life before a light hologram in hellish red descended from a projector hidden in the roof of the office. The picture flickered before revealing a hooded figure.

'What do you want?'

'My Lord, I am sorry to disturb your slumber but we have received news that a boy has been found within the ruin of the citadel.'

The hooded man leaned forward, his voice so sharp it could shred paper from 100 paces.

'What concern is that of mine?'

Everald gulped, his brow moistening.

'This was no refugee, Sir. As you might recall, we intercepted plans not long ago that rival Crimson and Blue factions were formulating to end the war.'

'Yes, a foolish notion.'

'Well, it looks like they might have succeeded…'

The hooded figure twitched in surprise.

'You have my attention, Sergeant.'

'In days of yore there was a prophecy that a child would be born of the red and blue inhabitants of this world; a child that would bring peace to our cause.

I believe that the prophecy has come true. We have isolated a young boy who we believe to be the one to bring Rodas together. Of course, this would mean the end of our campaign, Sir.'

'Churlish nonsense, Everald. Not one being in the known cosmos can stop the tide of the Crimson Empire.' The figure waved a skinless hand in the air, dismissing the Sergeant's claims.

Everald bit hard on his bottom lip before continuing. What he said next would put him in the direct line of fire from his superior.

'I'm sorry, Sir, but I believe that you may be wrong.'

The figure rose before him, eclipsing his form like a shadow.

'You'd better have a very good reason for your insubordination, Sergeant.'

'I do, Sir.' Everald shifted in his place, fists clenched so hard by his sides that his knuckles were turning white.

'And what proof do you have of this miracle child's existence?'

Everald wet his lips, his mouth gasping.

'He is purple.'

Instantly, the hooded man shot into life.

'DESTROY HIM!'

*

'Please remain calm. We just want to help you.'

The voice continued to buzz through the megaphone in a clam yet authoritative manner.

The child of Rodas stayed close to the floor, cowering from the strangers in a dark, desolate land. And then, he started paying attention to the voices in his head.

The man and woman's soothing tones somehow gave him strength. He could feel his resolve growing, his confidence blooming, and his eyes opening. The boy unfurled his ball-like form and gazed deep into the search light. All of a sudden, a wash of composure engulfed his very being, flooding his veins with a godly power. He slowly straightened his posture and met the harsh gaze of the heli-fighter's halogen search light.

'Please do not move. I repeat, do not move. We just want to help you.' As the Sacrificial Lamb looked down upon the child, he sensed that all was not in his power.

The purple boy walked towards the heli-fighter.

'Stay where you are!' the voice through the megaphone grew tense and desperate. To everyone's surprise aboard the vessel, the boy spoke.

'Why?'

'Why what?'

'Why should I stay where I am? You're not my Mum! At least, I hope not!'

The Sacrificial Lamb could hardly believe his ears. He could talk? There was something fishy in these duty ruins; and it wasn't the basic ingredients of his tuna sandwiches!

'Of...of course not. Just stay where you are.'

'Change the channel, Mumsy. I'm not going to do what anybody tells me.'

'If you don't we shall have no other alternative but to use force.'

'You'll have to come down here and catch me first!'

As the last syllable left the boy's mouth, a shower of electric rain shocked his body into submission. The defiant stature was replaced by crippling pain that sent him crumbling to the floor again. The boy screamed as the blue light sparked around him. The Sacrificial Lamb had deployed his energy net, which was normally used to round up enemies and refugees when the Crimson Empire were on patrol searching for prisoners. Now he had caught a new breed of Rodasian – a brand new, potentially dangerous manifestation. Images of promotions, interviews and chat show appearances danced in his head. His dreams of notoriety – for all the right reasons – were about to be dashed.

'Sir, I'm having trouble retaining altitude.' The heli-fighter pilot screamed back to the Private. He was right.

The Sacrificial Lamb could feel the whole craft begin to sink towards the ground. It was like the air beneath them had turned into quicksand.

The cockpit – which was big enough to fit five people – the pilot, co-pilot, two soldiers and himself, started to tip on its side. The Private lost his balance and fell against the window pane, dropping his megaphone in the process.

He blinked through the misty glass, his cold breath already forming a thick cloud of condensation. Through which, he could see what was causing this sudden turn of events. Down below, though not so far away as he had been, was the boy. Only now, he was on his feet, the energy net still shimmering electric blue, only the boy did not seem afflicted.

Although his whole body felt like it was being crippled by the force of the net, the boy was not letting on. He had rose to his feet – albeit with a struggle – and mustered enough power to pull on the net cord, which was still attached to the heli-fighter. His face grimaced and his teeth grinded as he pulled on the cord, it's taut, spring-like composition groaning against the weight of the craft.

The boy continued to muster super-Rodasian strength.

'Pull up, gadzukit!'

'I can't, Sir, the engines are starting to cut out. Anymore power and they will collapse under the pressure.'

The Sacrificial Lamb began struggling desperately for the megaphone. He now had his two soldiers crushing him against the glass panel. After a second or two scrambling with his one-free-hand, he clutched it to his crushed face.

'Let us go this instant!'

The boy couldn't believe what he had heard. Let them go?

'Do you really want me to do that?'

'For zargs sake, yes!'

The boy, his body still wracked with pain but refusing to give in to the sheer agony the net had encapsulated him in, stared deep into the whites of the eyes of the Private and pulled the heli-fighter down the last few remaining inches until all that separated the boy and the crew were the glass panels on the cockpit.

'...You're the boss.' He conceded as he let go of the cord.

The boy witnessed the panic in the Sacrificial Lamb's eyes as the heli-fighter, the energy net and the crew within shot off like a rocket up into the neon night sky, hurtling past the highest citadel tower before neatly sling-shotting out of the local vicinity all together before coming to a

firey halt, roughly five-hundred-yards away in a crumpled heap of metal and ruin.

The boy felt the pain ebb away from his aching muscles. He stood on the spot, panting for a brief moment, taking in all that had just happened. It was incredible. He had been born into this world with the strength of ten men - despite his outward appearance - he had a fully-functioning vernacular and he had just managed to outwit an entire crew of what looked like a band of tight-suited kidnappers...all with no clothes on!

'Oh, boy!' he muttered before covering up his pride. He huddled against a ruined wall and formulated his next cause of action. It would be daring, but he knew he could be successful, nonetheless. He would have to steal a ship and get off this godforsaken hell hole…and more vitally, find some clothes before he caused more of a scene than he had already cultivated!

VI

The news of the boy's escape was met with the anger of a thousand volcanos erupting at once – and that was just in Everald's office. His screams of frustration shattered the glass cube that was his office and burst every headset within a 100-yard-radius. With a crash, he pushed his way through what remained of his decimated office doors and stormed into the operations room.

'Get me all units. I want every man we can afford to converge on the child. I demand that every foot soldier, wild walker, heli-fighter and heli-carrier within a five-click range give that little son of a pillard everything we can. The boy is dangerous. He could mean the end of this war and the end of the mighty Crimson Empire. I don't care how many men we lose, I don't give a damn whether the enemy take advantage of the situation and meet us head-on, we have to stop the boy!'

Blood-red droplets of spittle showered onto the floor as the communication operators worked feverishly to send the orders out to every soldier available.

Meanwhile, as the activity around the citadel started to gather a-pace, the child had already managed to sneak his way out of the spotlight. He had found some strips of cloth lying tattered and torn in what looked like a long-forgotten market stall and formed a rudimentary t-shirt and trouser combination out of the tatty remains. He had even had enough spare material to make shoes – although the harder-than-usual skin on the souls of his feet had been impervious to the sharp shards of shrapnel he had trundled over so far. For now, he was out of the spotlight and had managed to cover his form in a much more dignified way than the 'tackle out' look he had been promoting not long earlier.

With the t-shirt pulled up over his face, covering his features, he walked at a brisk pace away from the horror of the citadel and further into the slums of the blue side of Rodas.

On his travels, he saw more misery than anyone should ever see in a lifetime. Homes had been destroyed beyond recognition, leading to an abundance of dirty, homeless people living on the streets. Men, women and children were fighting for shelter, scraps of food and fuel.

The look of desperation and helplessness bore into his soul. He tried to make sense of it all. What had started such a terrible atrocity?

Who would even consider leaving the people of this planet in such a terrible situation, where famine, pestilence, death and war ran rife.

Moreover, why did he have a lingering sensation within his mind that he was the one to help them? He couldn't even help himself and didn't even know who he was!

The boy held his head down and decided he could take no more. He kept his eyes straight, looking squarely at his feet on the path he trod and walked until he could not muster another step.

Finally, his breathing heavy and his legs feeling like lead pipes in quicksand, he collapsed to the ground. The first thing he noticed after rubbing his calves free of cramp was that the texture of the pavement had changed to sand. The coarse, fine grains filtered through his toes as he flexed his muscles. After mustering up the courage, he looked up again. The citadel was far, far behind him; so far, in fact, that the crumbled ruin was not anywhere to be seen. He was - quite literally - in the middle of nowhere.

'Now what?' He muttered quietly to himself.

The boy surveyed his surroundings. Apart from the neon shining moon, no other light emitted from the sky. The temperature had dropped almost to freezing, which would be deadly to any other Rodasian, but to the super boy, it was but a light chill.

'I suppose I could stay here for a while, take it all in. But where do I start? What the hell is going on? Why am I here? What's my name? And why the flicking gip am I talking to myself!' he laughed. As if his day hadn't been terrible already, he was considering a plea of insanity – maybe it would help in all this madness!

'Excuse me.'

The boy jumped out of his shiny, purple skin. He surveyed his surroundings. He was sure it was only himself in the vicinity and allowed himself to believe he was going mad.

A few moments passed before the nervous, pleading voice repeated itself.

'Excuse me, young fella. But would you mind awfully not treading on my face.'

The boy shrieked. He leapt from his spot and jolted to his left.

'Now you're on my shoulder.'

He sprung in the air again and again like a spring going insane in a supermarket trolley being pushed down a ten-storey stairwell.

'Look, now you're standing on my back. Please do try to be a little more consid..OOF! definitely not there! What's wrong with you, boy!' the voice seemed to be coming from directly below him.

'Who keeps saying that?' he asked.

'Mmmfff dumpf nufff puff.'

'What!?'

'I fed. Wud You Pleaff get off my faifff.'

The boy flung himself five feet to the left and rolled down a slight small sand dune. He could have sworn it was the voices in his head again.

'Thank you, that's better.'

He looked up over the dune and before his eyes, he witnessed a clump of sand collate together and form slowly into the shape and mass of a humanoid. The legs, torso, arms, neck and cranium all shifted and blurred in a sandy wave before turning to face him.

'W-who are you?'

'I'd have thought that was bleeding obvious - I am the Sandman.'

VII

The man made of granular substance towered over the boy. He stammered, in awe of what he had just seen.

'Y. Yur. You're.'

'Made of sand, yes. Tell me about it.'

'But, how?'

'How? I'll tell you how! I was once a proud man. A soldier by the name of Nethi Gaugman. I was a member of the 44th field battalion of the Sapphire Regime. I had it all; a rank of Commander and a group of men who would literally crawl across the biggest burning sun with their flies undone if I had ever given the order! And I would have done the same for them.'

The pair's eye-contact was broken momentarily as the boy tried to picture such an act of devotion in his head.

'Like so many others in my regiment, I had seen so much bloodshed and so much pain. As the war raged, I started to get itchy feet. So, I decided to apply for a special commissions unit that the Sapphire Regime installed. What really happened to me was far from what I expected…and so devastating it changed my life forever.'

The boy could sense a deep sincere feeling of betrayal and bitterness within the Sandman's speech pattern. It was growing by the second.

'They used me. I was an experiment! They changed my genetic make-up, stripped my Rodanity bare and spliced what I used to be until there was nothing left! They said I was going to be the first of a new line of soldiers - the leader of an infantry that could blend in with its surroundings and spy on our Crimson enemies without detection. I became a joke. The machine that they used upon me was faulty. My body's molecules became corrupt and what had once been made of flesh and bone became bonded with the grains of sand that scattered the floor of the laboratory. Later, I went on to find out that the operation was so experimental, so illegal, that the high command of the Sapphire Regime had absolutely no idea that these kinds of experiments were taking place.'

'So what did you do?'

'What any other self-respecting soldier would do. I fell apart!'

The boy was curious. 'What do you mean 'fell apart'?

'I crumbled. Both physically and mentally. The surgeons tried to move my crumbling body but when the nurses went to pick me up, my forearms fell through their fingers like…'

'Sand?'

The Sandman craned his grainy neck down to the boy.

'You guessed it. The next moment I was on the floor. And what did the scientists do to help me in my desperate predicament? They swept me up with a dust pan and brush! The main fella, this gangly looking berk who looked like his father was made of spaghetti and talked like he was forever trying to swallow a live cat, tried to explain aside what had happened – I heard his every word.

'It was nothing to do with him – he has warned that this machine was just a prototype and that he couldn't explain what had just happened. In the end, they swept me up, put my dusty remains in a jar and placed me on the shelf of the head scientist's office.

'In the end, I was still alive and my conscience was clear. I managed to shake what was left of my mutated form hard enough to knock the jar off its perch and I managed, with the will of my mind, to drag the contents to a nearby drain and escape. You see, I'd heard from meetings in that office that they wanted to attempt to reanimate my remains and give the experiment another go.

'But I ran away. I mean, what next? What is lower than a grain of sand?

A spec of dirt!? Ever since then, I've been a fugitive, trying my hardest to assemble my true form, again using nothing but willpower.'

The boy felt terrible but accepted that he and his new friend shared something in common.

'So, we're both fugitives then.'

'What are you wanted for?'

'I honestly don't know. I've been running ever since I can remember.'

'Which side are you on?' The Sandman enquired.

'Side?'

'Oh come on, what were you born five minutes ago?'

'More like ten,' said the boy.

The Sandman rather flippantly dismissed this retort.

'Well, as you should know, there are two sides to this war. The Crimson and the Sapphire. I can't tell which you are as I am colour blind. Not a side effect of my accident, more a problem I encountered when I suffered an explosion to the face in the great battle of Trevelyan.'

'I'm sorry, but could we get out of here? It's starting to get very cold and unless you can't see this too, I've only got a sheet on me!'

The Sandman subsided a little into the sand and lowered himself to the boy's level, his eye line peaking just under the child's spiky hair.

'Oh yeah, sorry I would have offered you a full quota of clothes but it's been so long since I spoke to anybody and as I don't wear clothes anymore, I hadn't noticed! Come inside.'

'What do you mean?' The boy surveyed the entire area. There was nothing at all but fine, tall hills of sand as far as the eye could see.

'Oh, hang on.'

The Sandman turned his back to the boy and inhaled greatly before letting out a breath so strong that a great hurricane blew from the figure. The wind roared and roared. The sand in front of him lifted like a film or a page turning.

'Bleedin' heck!'

The boy stood aghast. There, in front of him, was a grand spaceship, hidden in a hole in the ground.

IX

'Here is my home. Meet the Venus II. The fastest fighter-ship this side of the cosmos. It can do 0-60 in the speed of light. She's a baby at forty-two years old.'

The boy marveled at the brilliant craft.

'Come on in. I'd put the kettle on but I can't as I can no longer pick anything up without crumbling into a puddle of sand! Open.'

Instantly, a metal gantry descended from the belly of the ship, yawning open and revealing a bright light from within the ship. It made sense for the ship to be voice activated, especially as this slightly odd 'Sandman' fella insisted that it was almost physically impossible for him to touch things. The boy walked up into the Venus II and gasped in awe of its contents.

He was met by the sight of gleaming metal, shiny panels grinning ear-to-ear. If the Venus II were a house, then this would only be considered the hallway! He surveyed his surroundings deeper, taking a closer look at every aspect of the craft. In all his life, which was still in its immediate infancy, he could never have dreamed up such a thing of beauty.

The hallway was roughly a hundred metres in

length and further down the corridor there appeared to be doors branching off into other sections of the ship. With great enthusiasm, the boy asked his new friend if he could take a look around and proceeded to inspect the Venus.

After several minutes he had found what looked like a hospitality area, complete with a kitchen and a seating area for people to relax.

The boy heard a slinking sound behind him which indicated that the Sandman had joined him.

'How long have you had this thing?'

'Oh, a few years, I guess. This old girl didn't cost me a thing. You could say I stole it. It's wanted by the Crimson Empire. You see, it used to be there until my regiment snatched it from right under their noses. Then, just days before my accident, I was entrusted with hiding it somewhere inconspicuous and I chose out here. Quite ironic, really isn't it considering what ended up happening to me!'

'If it's called the Venus II then what happened to the Venus I?'

The Sandman went on to regale the boy with the story of the original Venus craft. Roughly 70 years ago, a decorated war hero by the name of Sveto Rolansky designed and built a ship so vast yet designed and built a ship so vast yet so nimble and powerful, that the Sapphire Regime decided to finance his plans and turn it from what was supposed to be a cruise liner into a warship.

The Government had enthused that the hospitality features should remain in the plans, but unfortunately, the original idea to have a swimming pool had to be sacrificed for an abundant array of all variations of armoury instead. Rolansky, after much deliberation and protest, eventually yielded but insisted that he be placed in charge of its construction and would also hold the distinction of test piloting the craft when it was ready.

After nearly twenty years had passed, the ship was set to sail on its maiden voyage. People from around the blue hemisphere gathered in their millions to see its maiden voyage, which was to include a handbrake turn around the seven moons of Hox before reversing into the Royal Chamber of Queen Troxby of Flom on the neighbouring planet of Dup. However, it was to go terribly, terribly wrong.

'...Y'see, there was a tiny design flaw. Just as Rolansky was about to apply the handbrake turn he had a moment of realisation.'

'What? There wasn't enough petrol to get back?' The boy asked.

'No, there was no handbrake.' The Sandman replied. 'Smashed straight into the first moon of Rox and that was that. Total muck up on his part. That's the trouble with us Rodasians. We sometimes miss the smallest detail and that can cause massive devastation because for Rolansky it cost him his life. Still, I've heard stories that the man was, not only a pacifist, which is libbing hard on this planet, but also a consummate thief too. You see, his initial idea for this ship was taken from a colleague of his after a heavy nights drinking in the notorious pub district of this planet. But because he had laced his friend's drink with a chemical agent that wiped his memory and sadly left him a gibbering vegetable, he would never be taken to court and sued for stealing the original idea. Then again, Rolanksy certainly got his comeuppance. It had the biggest television audience this side of our galaxy. It even went on to win the vote for the funniest moment in the history of Ursa-17.'

'So, how do you fly this thing? I mean, you must have got it out here somehow.'

The Sandman lurched his head to the sand, making tiny granules of his being seemingly fall out of his left ear.

'I was lucky enough to discover that one of the AI prototypes was on board at the time - no idea why.'

'AI?'

'Artificial Intelligence. Both sides of this war have been developing them in a bid to stop the death of so many foot soldiers. The process was in its infancy when I ran away but this little guy was a highly advanced test run to allow inanimate objects to come alive and carry out useful jobs for the war effort. Come here, pet!'

The pair glanced up towards the hallway and heard the clattering of metal upon metal from afar. With great speed, the sound became louder and louder. The boy's mind raced as to what this AI must be? A robot-man? Whatever it was, it sounded powerful and it was heading straight for them.

In a flash, a blur of silver shot past the fugitives around ankle height, blowing both the boy to the ground and the Sandman into hundreds of pieces.

Gingerly, both got to their feet and whilst the Sandman assembled himself again in a rather frustrated manner, the boy took in the being that had now joined them.

'Skateboard, I've told you before, you really must run a diagnostic on your speed setting, it's far too fast still! I don't want another situation like last time, when I asked you to clean the kitchen and you shot straight through the hull wall!'

'Apologies, Sir.' A sharp, metallic yet friendly voice emitted from a small gap in the top of the robot. The boy grinned at what he saw. The AI was thin, very thin. It had the same depth as a flat packed piece of cupboard. The robot also ran on four little wheels and its back - or body depending on how you looked at it - was three feet in length. There were no eyes or ears to speak of and the boy's reflection shone in the sparkling metal finish.

'Skateboard meet…I'm sorry I don't even know your name?'

The boy looked startled. His life had been so hectic and unconventional that he hadn't had time to stop and think of a name for himself. He had a nagging feeling that the naming of a new person was the job for somebody else, not he! He raced through his fervent memories and settled upon a name that befitted his rather unorthodox early moments.

'Random.' He said. 'My name is Random.'

'It's a pleasure to make your acquaintance, Sir', Skateboard chirped. 'Would you like some tea, brewed from the finest milk of the Utup seed?' Random hesitated.

'Sure. What does it taste like?'

'How should I know… I don't have any taste buds.'

Skateboard retreated to the kitchen bay as the Sandman beckoned Random towards the cockpit. If the rest of the Venus II had the majestic splendour of a Royal barge, then the cockpit had all the charm of a back alley outside a gentleman's club at four in the morning.

It was dark, dank and smelly and housed four chairs, all with control panels in front, and one steering wheel to the left of the front nose that the cockpit was situated in. It was also relatively cramped. Random thought it would be rude of him to ask why this part of the ship felt so incomplete to the rest of it, until the Sandman answered his question for him, as if he were inside his head.

'Cut backs,' he admitted.

He beckoned for Random to take a seat in the pilot's chair. And then, licking his lips like sandpaper, he asked the crunch question.

'Do you reckon you know how to fly this thing?'

'Definitely not,' Sandman admitted.

'But you could be taught. It's very simple you know. Think of it like driving a small shuttle car.'

'But I've never driven one of those either.'

The Sandman grew impatient and snapped at his new guest.

'Is there anything you can do?'

'Well…apparently I can drag heli-fighters down to the ground using nothing but my strength.'

The Sandman roared with laughter.

'Don't you play games with me, boy. I've already told you that I can't touch anything. I need someone to pilot this thing for one last special mission.'

Random did not like the tone of his voice or the direction that the conversation was heading.

'What's that then?'

'The Sapphire Regime destroyed my life. They took away who I was, what I stood for, everything I achieved with no possibility of returning to the life I once had.'

'You could always just ask them to fix things?'

'I'm a soldier, Random. We don't ask questions.'

Random started to shift uneasily in his chair.

'What are you asking of me?'

'I want you to take me to the headquarters of the Sapphire Regime and destroy the last strong post that they have got…and everyone within…'

X

'That's murder!'

Random looked back at the Sandman with an expression of utter disgust. Was there no decent being on this god forsaken planet he lived upon?

'That's war.' The Sandman's retort was cold and final. 'Every soul on this planet knows how long this war has raged. Are you seriously telling me that not all of us have taken a life at some point in our miserable, futile lives?'

'Not me.' Random stopped sharply after his statement. He thought back to the Sacrificial Lamb, the electric netting and the way in which he launched that heli-fighter full of soldiers off into the night sky. A feeling of shame passed through his bones as if an army of ghosts were walking along his spine. Surely, that didn't make him a killer too?'

Confused and distressed, he buried the feeling deep down.

'Oh, I see your conscience is working, isn't it? So you have taken a life. Then, how is this any different?'

'And then what?' Random spat. 'We become fugitives? Wanted by the Sapphire Regime for the rest of eternity?'

'You're forgetting. We are in the Venus II. We

can jump to any part of the galaxy. Anywhere at all – and they'd never find us. And, even if they ever did catch up with us, we'd just hop away again.'

'I don't want to live my life forever looking over my shoulder,' said Random. 'I've not been here long and I refuse to become a war criminal just to help you out.'

'Well, the way I see it is that you've got three choices. Either you do as I ask, escape Rodas and build a new life elsewhere. Or, you can get off my ship right now and I'll leave you to whoever you're running from.'

'And the third?'

Why did I ask that? Random mused. He already knew what the other alternative was.

'Or I kill you right now.'

Random gulped hard. What kind of a world was this? Red and blue men and women? A man made entirely out of sand? A talking Skateboard!? He needed to get away, safely. Although he knew deep down that this was his true home and his purpose was here. But he didn't want it. He would do anything to escape this madness. Anything.

'Okay. It doesn't seem like I have a choice then, does it?' he conceded. 'I'll pilot you to the headquarters of the Sapphire Regime. All I ask in return is that after what's done is done, that you leave me somewhere far from here and we never come face to face again.'

The Sandman shot a sinister smile. 'Deal. Well, I'll leave you in the capable hands of Skateboard. He'll show you the ropes. Of course, whilst you're here, you'll not be allowed to leave the ship.'

'Why would I want to?' Random said. He was right. It was a safe haven, hidden miles from anywhere. He knew he was in a good place, but how to get away with his life? Random now knew that this guy was nuts. Of course he was. After such a traumatic experience as having his own personal being changed so immeasurably, that was enough to send anyone mad and vengeful considering he wanted to kill those that had wronged him. An eye-for-an-eye, as it were.

'Skateboard will look after you. And if you DO try to escape, I won't.'

Random gulped hard.

'You're the boss.'

*

Random spent the next two days as the guest to this non-massed psychopath. He was clothed, fed and watered and spent his time studying the ship. The Sandman had not been present during this time as he seemed more at home in the sand dunes outside the Venus II.

So instead, Random, dressed in a canary yellow t-shirt with khaki full-length trousers and smart, polished black boots, was left with the company of Skateboard, who was acting more as his personal guard more than anything else. Using tact, he was learning – piece-by-piece – everything about the Venus that the weird AI had to offer. After a while, he felt like he had begun to build a trust with the robot. Enough to ask the question he had been burning to ask since he had agreed to do the Sandman's deed.

On a trip to the engine room, which was just as dank and dirty as the cockpit itself, Random saw his chance.

'Have you ever killed anyone Skateboard?'

The little robot stopped in his tracks.

'I do not know what you mean, Sir.'

'Y'know. Have you ever taken a life?'

'Why would you ask me that?'

'It's just that I thought that if you have been in the service of this Sandman fella for a while you might share his vision of destruction, that's all.'

Skateboard hesitated.

'I'm hurt by your presumption, if you don't mind me saying so.'

Random was surprised.

'Hurt? But you're a robot.'

'I may not be organic like yourself Sir, but I can still feel.'

There was awkward silence between the two for a couple of clicks.

'Just because I serve the Sandman, it doesn't mean that I want to help him. Why do you think I made a hole in the hull when the Sandman brought it up?'

'Because your speed setting is on the blink?'

'No. I was trying to escape.'

Random began to feel empathy with the item.

'The master found me on this ship but I am not his. I was built to help ship goods and supplies to the refugee camps that the Sapphire Regime held. I was helping out those members of the Crimson Empire that had been captured and were being held against their will.'

'Then how on earth did you end up here?'

Skateboard pulled himself up against the shin bones of Random, like a dog seeking attention. Instinctively, Random began to pat Skateboard, tentatively at first, to reassure him.

'There was a severe vehicle shortage that led to the Venus being assigned to make a short trip to the camps as our old freighter was severely damaged in a bombardment. So, I and my fellow androids loaded the ship up with fresh supplies ready for transport. We of the Sapphire side may be just as culpable for this war, but it doesn't mean that we butcher the prisoners we keep. Then, just as I was loading the bay on board, the Sandman came aboard. Only he wasn't made of sand then. Since his regiment had been given orders to take the Venus for their own, he piloted the ship out here, forgetting that I was still on board. He landed the Venus in a crater and locked me inside. The next time I saw him he was totally different. No longer a man with skin and bones; instead his body had been replaced with sand. I was perplexed. He spotted me in my hiding space down here and threatened to destroy me if I didn't help him out. I've been here ever since, doing his will. Not out of pity or want, but out of fear.'

'You know he is easy to disable. He has no physical mass. It would be easy to pass through him!'

Skateboard shook his body. 'Yes, I know, but sand gets everywhere. He could easily clog my instruments and then I'd be powerless, scrap even!'

Random stroked his new found friend with more tenderness than before.

'I can help you.'

'How?' enquired Skateboard.

'We can team up. Get rid of this Sandman guy and then we can escape. That way, we don't have to kill anyone and we get shot of both our captor and this terrible planet.'

Skateboard mulled the idea over in his mainframe.

'But where would we go?'

Random smiled.

'Anywhere. We can go anywhere in the galaxy. You and I. Skateboard and Random and the Venus II. What do you say?'

'I like the sound of that, Sir.' If Skateboard had a mouth he would have been grinning from ear-to-ear.

'Good boy,' Random patted his companion. 'Now, do you know how to pilot this thing?'

'I do. But although this ship is compatible with my sensors I am unable to do so.'

'Why?'

'No hands.' Skateboard wiggled to elaborate his point. 'Plus, I can't reach the steering wheel! My frame is not very complimentary, especially in height!'

'Okay, not to worry,' Random assured. 'Teach me and I'll get us out of here.'

And so, with the attack on the Sapphire Regime's HQ imminent, Random and Skateboard set about formulating their plan of escape - for they both knew that this was their only chance to flee Rodas, and the murderous desires of the Sandman for good.

XI

When the big day arrived, Random was exhausted. He had inadvertently lost the ability to sleep the night before. He stirred and shook in his bunk, which had been prepared for him by Skateboard. It was meticulously pristine; it gleaned in the night light and even though he was wearing a face mask, Random was still blinded by the neon moon. Its reflection bounced around the clean metal walls and shone in his eyes so brightly, he was genuinely worried for his sight the next morning.

For three whole weeks afterwards, he swore he was seeing everyone in an entirely different spectrum altogether. The two previous nights, Random had slept down in the engine room with Skateboard, whose only luxury was a tiny basket which he slept in with a canister of oil by its side in case he got stiff in the night. Although it was small and dark, Random had enjoyed his rest time down there.

It was a shame that he was moved, for appearances sake, just so that they did not arouse suspicion regarding their conspiracy to take over the Venus II.

He had spent all day trying to master the complex instruments of the ship in preparation for the attack on the HQ.

The Sandman came in from the harsh sand every now and then to see the progress his "captive" was making.

In the back of his grainy little mind, the Sandman had a feeling that his obedient pet was working behind his back; that the robotic drone was trying to help this strange boy to escape anyway he could. However, as his short term memory dwindled as quickly as the sands of time would blow, he kept departing back to the dunes before having the exact same nagging feeling of paranoia and coming back to check on his unwilling co-conspirators again.

There had been one occasion upon which Random had asked what the entire plan was, but the Sandman was keeping his cards close to what used to be his chest and informed the Sandman that information was on a "need to know basis, which was not needed at present".

All of this cloak and dagger had infuriated Random; he was frustrated beyond belief. He wanted to know all the ins and outs so that he and Skateboard could counter act it with little difficulty.

As he lay in bed, blinded by the night-time light, he worried that whatever he and his robotic accomplice would do, the Sandman may be able to stop them. And what could the Sandman do to him? Turn him into a sand storm and suffocate him? As far as Random was concerned, the Sandman was an unknown entity.

He had been a soldier before his experiment had gone wrong so what did that warped mind have in store? Random's mind tossed and turned. He had never felt so nervous and unsure, especially given that there were still the questions surrounding his own existence. The voices in his head had stopped - for now - but their requests had nagged at his conscience. He knew that he had something very important to do, but what? Save the planet? Find his parents?

Even if he were able to fall into a deep slumber, he was still haunted by the first scenes he remembered witnessing. Death and devastation. That laboratory room, the fire, disease and helpless refugees he had walked past. How could he have helped them even if he knew how? He needed guidance, a clear head and a new beginning, even if his own was only a few days previously. He needed to get away.

On the morning of the attack, Random was awoken by the ship alarm, blazing through the speaker systems like razorblades through marshmallow. The klaxon wailed mercilessly for what seemed like an eternity and sent Random scurrying to the ground, his hands to his ears.

Eventually, the klaxon blared no more and was replaced with the voice of the Sandman.

'Wakey wakey!' he screamed. 'Today's the day, young man. Meet me up in the hospitality area in ten clicks flat!'

Random panted, his heart beating furiously. He scrambled around the bed, clawing for his belongings, trying to remember everything Skateboard had taught him. He could remember their plan to dispose of the Sandman but how to fly mere metres off the ground and loop whilst firing photon torpedoes at the same time, well that required revision most horrid! Nevertheless, and despite his fatigue, lack of sight and now bleeding ear drums, he stood defiantly and strode on his way out of his room towards his fate.

When he got to the hospitality area, he found that a place had been laid for him at the dining table, accompanied with fresh juice and a bowl of cereal. The Sandman stood tall and proud next to a video screen that had descended from the ceiling and Skateboard stood next to him, as obedient as ever.

'You took your time. Come on! There isn't a moment to spare.'

'Alright, alright, I'm here now, aren't I?'

Random sneered, his retort like that of a petulant teenager.

The Sandman snorted. 'I hope that Skateboard has been of some use to you these last few days. I saw his tutorials that you took part in. I hope that they were of help.'

The last sentence was more of a statement and less of a question, thought Random so he kept quiet as he tucked into his breakfast.

'Now, you may be wondering why we shall be attacking the Sapphire Regime during the day time? Well, as you'll realise, the army is most tired at the start of the day due to the brightness of our moon, making them an easier target at the start of a new day and tactically less aware. Also, as you will now realise, the Venus II is so fast and nimble it can shake off the most stubborn of heat seeking missiles and is also blessed with a cloaking device.'

The video screen fizzed into life and showed a detailed layout of the Sandman's target. His right finger elongated into a pointer stick and indicated along with his instructions.

'So what we shall do, is fly the two hundred miles to the HQ, fly in from the west, as you can see that side of the complex is less protected from fire arms than others and whilst the shield bubble can protect it from a heavy bombardment, as we are but one ship, I shall send an energy pulse that will disable anything electronic within a hundred metres of us so that we can fly in, deploy our bombs and fly out again. This pattern we shall have to repeat four times, once for every side of the complex. After this, we shall fly up to the tip of the HQ and drop one last thermal detonator on the main offices of the HQ, wiping out the chain of command and leaving the Sapphire Regime crumbling and weaker than ever before.'

Random raised his hand whilst stuffing his mouth with cereal with the other.

'Yes?' the Sandman said wearily.

'Excuse me for asking,' Random spat through his mouthful, 'But won't that mean that the Crimson Empire will just end up taking over the planet?'

'Exactly! And then the war will finally be over. My revenge will be exacted and Rodas shall be free once more.'

'But I've seen the Crimson Empire at work. They tried to kill me. If anything you've said is to go by, they seem a hundred times worse than your lot. So, why after all these years of fighting for the Blue Army are you allowing the reds to win?'

He had a point, thought the Sandman. If only the boy knew the hurt and suffering that his own kind had put him through, he'd want to kill them too.

'When your own kinds have turned their backs on you, you have no choice but to turn yours on them.'

Random chewed enthusiastically as he listened on. He was putting on a façade; not wanting to let his captor on that he was actually plotting his downfall.

'As soon as HQ is in flames, we shall then make our escape. Under the cover of our cloaking device, you shall then pilot us out of this system, past the blockades on the planet's outer rim and when that final hurdle of security is past, set co-ordinates for the furthest planet on the furthest reach of the galaxy and we shall wait for the heat to die down.'

'But I thought you said that you'd drop me off at the next possible opportunity? We had a deal!'

The Sandman smiled maniacally. 'If you get us out of this, I won't want you out of my sight. You'll be far too valuable to me, I'm afraid. Eventually, you shall help me assume a new body.'

Random shivered. He knew what those words meant.

He wanted to steal his body, if he had the chance. More determined than ever, Random was going to have to stay on his toes, stick to the plan he and Skateboard had made and get rid of the maniac for good!

'Now eat up, Mr Random. We commence the attack in 20 clicks!'

'Don't worry,' Random sneered as he washed his cereal down with a final gulp of fruit juice. 'I'm ready now.' He slammed the glass back down on the table, pushed his chair back and made his way to the cockpit, observed intensely by Skateboard and the Sandman all the way.

*

The next twenty clicks passed by like hours. A knot had formed in Random's chest and it burned with anxious heat. He had been a little too hasty in his enthusiasm to 'get-on' with the job in hand and had been told by the Sandman that they would stick to that time frame as there was a window of opportunity in timing as the Crimson Empire's attack would cease momentarily in the window. When they were ready, Random piloted the Venus II with alarming ease - either Skateboard was a fantastic tutor or he had a natural talent.

Nevertheless, he kept his eyes front of the house and maintained his concentration on the job in hand. With a click of a button, the starter motor snarled into life. The entire ship juddered along to the rhythm of the engine and his cheeks waddled up and down as he raised his steering wheel. The Venus II shuddered up from its hiding place in the sand dune and shot up through the coating of sand that disguised it, into the fresh air. The brightness of the Rodas sun illuminated the cockpit and Random had to fetch for a pair of goggles that sat serupticiously on the dashboard. He couldn't quite believe it, he was flying!

This moment of triumph was short-lived as his mind returned to the task in hand. He and Skateboard had decided to fly as close as they could to the HQ before it became impossible for them to escape the warring mire just so the Sandman's suspicions were not aroused.

Then, on Random's command, Skateboard, who was blue toothed into the network, requested all the doors and windows be opened on board so that the Sandman's body was to be sucked out of the craft and trapped on Rodas for good. It was a simple and effective plan, thought Random.

However, it all hinged on one or two technical errors coming into place. The previous evening, unbeknownst to their captor, Skateboard had managed to integrate with the firewall matrix and deactivated the Sandman's voice activation capabilities and instructed the main frame computer to switch users when instructed to do so. Otherwise, the doors would never open. Random crossed his toes that his robotic friend's calculations had been successful.

They were nearing the HQ with alarming velocity. This ship really knew how to move, thought Random! At less than two clicks away, the time was almost right to dump the Sandman for good.

'Nearly there now,' observed the Sandman. 'Just don't try anything funny now. Or I'll choke you.'

Random nodded his head in acknowledgement.

'No problem.'

He gestured to Skateboard with a pre-agreed double blink that the time was now. Inside, the AI's mechanisms whirred and buzzed. The codes were snapping together and the binary systems were lining up.

Within a mini-second, they had connected with the firewall. But the doors refused to budge. Random shot a look of panic at his companion.

'Ah.' Skateboard said audibly. 'I forgot to carry the three!'

'What!?' The Sandman stared daggers of ice at his drone. 'What are you talking about?'

Random flipped the craft upside down. The Sandman's form hour glassed away from what had been the floor and then reformed on what was previously the ceiling.

'Traitors' he yelled, sending a huge dust cloud towards Random and Skateboard, who were fastened and electronically bolted to their places so they didn't fall like their captor.

Random saw the dust cloud heading straight for him, causing him to act by swinging the ship back on its belly and sending the Sandman hurtling down the hospitality area.

'For god's sake, Skateboard, can you fix the calculation?'

'Yes, Sir. But it'll take about four clicks. I'm sorry, long mathematics has never been my forte.'

'Now you tell me!' Random hollered as another sand cloud shot towards him, shaped like a giant hand of terror. He flipped the ship again, making himself feel a little queasy in the process.

And so their plan had failed to work. But worse was to come for the captives of the Sandman. A blip on the sonnerscope made Random's flesh crawl. They had entered the war zone. The Sandman's timing had been off…there was a battle raging on the outskirts of the HQ and they were flying straight into it…

XII

Random's training had failed to cover evasive maneuvers. It had also failed to include what to do when a shape shifting man made of sand is trying to kill you whilst you are simultaneously hurtling towards the heart of an interplanetary battle. The scene was horrific. Dozens upon dozens of small planes dog fighting in the sky before him, the searing energy weapons firing left right and centre. Try as he might, he couldn't turn the Venus II around.

Another jet of sand coursed its way towards the boy but the blast door leading to the cockpit snapped shut just before it threatened the pair.

'Sir, I've managed to hot wire the door mechanisms. He shouldn't give us any problems for the time being.'

Skateboard's tone was one of triumph. Random didn't share his enthusiasm.

'Now all we need to do is fly out of this hell hole!'

'Look out!' Skateboard's robotic tones shrieked as Random spotted out of the corner of his goggles a bolt of energy hurtling straight towards them. He dropped the steering shaft and the Venus ducked below the laser and out of harm's way.

But now Random was piloting the ship into a whole web of lasers and rockets. He slalomed through the worst of them, but the right wing of the Venus was scorched by a stray.

'That's close enough for me.' Random said. 'Skateboard, are you any closer to opening the cabin windows?'

'Nearly there, Sir. Hang on; my sensors have indicated that the Sandman is finding another way of getting in here.'

Random looked startled.

'How?'

'Through the air ducts.'

'Close the air conditioning system in here.'

'But Sir, you'll suffocate.'

'I'll hold my breath!' If there was one thing Random wasn't concerned with right now, it was his breathing! But it was too late. Tiny grains of sand began to trickle out of the vents in the dashboard and the cockpit walls. He was breaking through!

'Hold on, did you say that you had hotwired the door mechanisms?'

'That is correct, Sir.'

The expression on Random's face turned from one of stress to one of relief.

'Skateboard, open all the doors on board. Do it!'

The little robot obeyed and tripped the firewall again. Straight away the cockpit door shuddered open. The Sandman was waiting there, his tentacles made of grain were ballooning through all the air vents and now stood, vengeful, at a swollen height of eight feet and filled the doorway.

'You betrayed me. Now I'll make you suffer. I'm going to fill your lungs with sand until you gag your last breath.'

A sudden gust of wind roared mercilessly towards the cockpit.

'Guess again.'

Random had the last word as the Sandman, every last fragment of his being, was sucked out of the ship and scattered on the warring crafts below like ashes from an airplane.

They had done it.

The Sandman was gone. Now Random had to get them out of this crossfire before there was nothing left of either him or Skateboard.

The laser fire fizzed past the Venus II as it continued to dodge its way around the battlefront. Random used the steering console to twist past them, although he was still not comfortably at ease with the ship.

He had adapted quickly after just a couple of days of training from an artificial being that resembles a child's form of transport, but it was going to take some getting used to, if they ever escaped!

'Could you scan the area for the imperfection in the shield again?' he asked.

'I'll do it now, Sir. However, my synaptic connections are still connected to the ship, but in the wrong department. I don't suppose you could reach into my back and connect my external drive to the dashboard.'

'Um', Random stalled, as an explosion splintered in front of him. 'A bit busy here, Skateboard. Could you do it yourself?'

At this moment, a crisscross of warring heli-fighters sprang into action above the Venus.

Random glanced above and recognized the face of one of the co-pilots. It was the Sacrificial Lamb! True, he was looking a little worse for wear and from where he was sitting, Random could faintly see a white plaster secured over the bridge of his nose, a bloodied bandage around his forehead and two of his right arms in a sling. Embarrassed, Random gave him a nervous smile and waved.

'After him!' the soldier hissed to his crew, snapping his broken arms straight before recoiling again in blatant agony.

'This is about to get a bit rougher.' Random said as he slid the accelerator pedal further down to the floor.

Despite all the danger, he allowed himself a brief second to feel proud. He hadn't killed anyone when he escaped the Crimson Empire. His conscious was clear…and it would remain so.

Meanwhile, Skateboard was doing his best to lasso the external socket into the vacant 12 volt adapter in the dashboard of the ship. He tried using the momentum of the Venus' swing motion as it avoided the blaster fire to slot the connection home. But with the increased speed, it was becoming more and more difficult to succeed.

'Wait a minute, this is ludicrous. Skateboard, how fast can this thing go?'

'0-60 at the speed of light, Sir.'

'Then why can't we do it? I mean here we are in mortal danger and I've got my foot down and I can't be doing more than –' he looked at the speedometer, ' – 120 miles per hour!'

'Well, you couldn't be expected to handle a ship with that velocity, my young Sir. Your piloting experience is only eleven clicks and four semi-clicks old.'

'It doesn't matter.' The Venus began to shudder even more. The firepower from the heli-fighters was gaining. It was clear that they had identified Random as the fugitive.

And what's more, the fire was now concentrated on the sleek, stolen ship.

It had been identified as a property of the Sapphire Regime, making it desired by both parties.

'Those shots are getting closer. Give me visual.'

Random soon wished he hadn't made that last demand. Looking at the image on the scanner, he gulped hard. It was a miracle – the fighting had stopped, but now he had 400 crafts from both sides of the war bearing down upon him.

'Schparzos,' Random swore.

'Please, Sir. Just because I don't have ears, doesn't mean that I am not immune to coarse, offensive language.'

'Skateboard, I'm begging you. Please. We have to hit a faster speed. We have both sides of this war on our tails. I can't keep us safe for much longer.'

'Suggest evasive action.'

'Skateboard!' Random was becoming desperate.

'There's a one-mile hole in the oncoming blockade. Move five degrees to the right and slam on the breaks.'

'What! That's suicide!'

'Trust me.'

Random obeyed. He maneuvered the ship five degrees and pushed his left foot down as hard as he could.

The Venus shuddered to a grinding halt. Random felt the pressure of his action hold him firmly back in the pilot's chair. To his utter astonishment, all 400 vessels shot past his windscreen like horizontal bullets of rain and darted out of view. Thanks to the ingenious mind of his companion, they had bought a few seconds of time to escape. Random used his novice driving skills to carry out a swift three-point turn in the middle of the sky and zoom off in the opposite direction.

He overheard the clanking of metal and several small explosions over the intercom. Daring to explore the scanner again, Random noticed that the army of ships that were pursuing him had also attempted their maneuvers in a bid to continue the chase. Fortunately, due to the lack of space and their impatience to complete the about-turns professionally, the freight of Crimson and Sapphire soldiers had only succeeded in creating a near-400 ship pile-up.

Within moments, the majority of the crashed fighters began to drop like great boulders towards the ground, smashing in the harsh sand with all the subtle grace of a troop of pregnant dancing hippopotamus' falling through a cling-film floor into a collection of priceless vases.

'You see? Now you don't have to hit the speed of light to escape.' Skateboard's statement seemed almost triumphant. What the little AI was not telling his new friend, was that there was a slight fault in the ship's calibration system. He had been meaning to get around to fixing it, integrating himself with the matrix and finding the best solution, but the Sandman had been keeping him preoccupied with other things. Instead of an upkeep of maintenance, he had been nothing else but a pitiful dogs body. He knew that there was one more challenge that the minimal crew of the Venus II faced.

'Sir, before we go any further, I must respectfully request that we seek shelter somewhere and make some improvements. We are not out of the woods yet.'

Random checked his scanner again. The HQ, the fighters and the devastation was becoming nothing but a spec in the distance. 'We've cleared the danger zone. What are these "improvements" you are on about?'

Skateboard confessed that if they increased their current velocity then there was a very probable chance that the engines would explode as a by-product of the top speed being staunched.

'There's also one final obstacle in our route away from Rodas,' he said.

'On the outer perimeters of the planet there is a security net. A security net made up of an interlocking fence that is nearly impenetrable. There are some soldiers, but they are not affiliated with the Crimson Empire or the Sapphire Regime.'

'Then who do they work for?'

'The galaxy. This war has been raging for so long, even the history books of interstellar scholars cannot tie the precise date of its creation down. It's a total mystery, but it also highlights just how dangerous the rest of the cosmos views it. So, thc governments of Ursa-17, 18 and 19 decided to pool their efforts together and constructed a security mainframe that sealed over the planet. Both sides of Rodas knew; in fact, they reluctantly agreed to its construction. There was no point for the disease of our wretched world to spread across the universe. You've seen the devastation that we have lived with. Can you imagine the whole sector giving in to such horror?'

Random kept his eyes straight as the Venus cruised through the sand plains.

'So, what do we do?'

'We can break through the barrier but we will have to use the light speed at the precise second of the energy surge.

I've taken the liberty and conducted some research into the workings of the barrier and discovered that every 40 clicks an energy pulse fires along the netting, regenerating its containment fields. So, we can burst through the barrier much like we did with the force field the HQ trapped us in.'

'Speaking of which, how did we get out –?'

The ship crashed into an invisible force and its nose section bounced back several metres.

'I believe you have just found it, Sir.' Skateboard stated obtusely.

Random huffed as he picked himself up of the dashboard. They spent the next few moments trying to locate the hole they had entered through and when they did, they sailed off back into the wastelands from which they came.

Far below, as the Venus II flew away into the ether, a shimmering, pulsating life force disrupted the perfect sand dunes that surrounded the plain. Like molecules reconnecting, something which looked like waves began to pool together. And the tremor was growing. It was the Sandman, scattered like ashes ready to rise like a phoenix and reclaim what was rightfully his. After the betrayal of his two co-conspirators, he was going to stop at nothing until the Venus was his again…and the boy who claimed to be named Random was dead.

XIII

It took the two fugitives the equivalent of four earth hours to make the necessary repairs and upgrades. Not that Random was much help to the cause; unless there was a nut that needed tightening or a physical diagnostic that needed running, it was all Skateboard's doing. Although the Venus II was a state-of-the-art ship, equipped for battle or leisure requirements, it had needed a refurbishment – which prompted Random to ask the question.

'So, how long did the Sandman have it?'

Skateboard tutted to himself. Although he was a highly advanced AI machine, he like anybody else, did not entertain interruption. Especially when he was calibrating the new shield generator for four times its current strength and capacity.

'I'm not entirely certain, Sir. I was only in the Sandman's employment for what must have been a few months. He didn't speak much to me unless he wanted something. But I remember pouring through the security tapes one evening and noticed that he was deeply disturbed by his predicament.'

'How come?'

'Not that I want to sound unkind, even to him, but he wept to himself in his cabin at night and every time he went to wipe the tears away, he was inadvertently rubbing away a section of his face. He once cursed to me so ferociously that he let his pain show. "Imagine living inside a nightmare, where your skin is so coarse and uncomfortable to touch, to wear something so abrasive that it hurts to even breathe and to fall apart at the slightest breeze. To be robbed of your life, your dreams, your goals, your loved ones. To be shunned from existence as another of the galaxies mutated mysteries. Could you live with that?"

Random let the information sink in. No wonder the Sandman was so desperate to escape.

'So, he was driven to the extreme.'

'I think that his real intention was to find a cure. But he couldn't trust the Sapphire Regime. Not again. He was betrayed by them in ways that neither of us could ever understand. Deep down, I believe he was just looking for an out.'

'And we denied him that chance.' Random concluded.

Skateboard went back to his calibrations as his counterpart sighed heavily.

'Maybe we could have reasoned with him; made him see that if we worked together, we could all help one another?'

'At the end of the day, Sir, he was - nay - IS a soldier. A soldier in the bloodiest war the cosmos has ever known. He would do anything for revenge. If it had meant death, it would still have guaranteed him salvation. How do you bargain with a man like that?'

Random sighed, left the question unanswered and continued tightening the bolts on the Venus' shield array. The next few moments passed silently before Random disrupted Skateboard again; a move which led to the robot accidentally opening all the airlocks and turning on the ventilation shafts at the same time, improbably blowing nearly all the interior décor of the cabins into the mid-section of the ship, and an apologetic Random down tooling and tidying up the mess. After detecting a slight inkling that he may have been a distraction to his friend, he sluggishly picked himself up and plopped himself in the pilot's chair and fiddled with the levers and buttons until the irritable AI was finished. He also felt a keen duty to look after this ship, and keep an eye out for its previous owner. After the picture that Skateboard had painted so vividly, this wasn't the kind of person the duo wanted to run into again. He sat slumped in the comfortable chair and gazed out into the starry night.

The Venus had been on silent running ever since they escaped the HQ of the Sapphire Regime. At night, the ship's outer hull disguised itself in darkness, making it hard to detect to the naked eye. It had been coated in something called poli-carbite armour, making it near impregnable also. Random couldn't believe his luck.

Suddenly, he could hear the voices again in his head. At first the man's and then the woman's tones bled into audacity. He knew that they would be back again as soon as he had nothing to distract him. And now he was alone, and in relative safety, he listened to what they had to say.

'You alone are the one who can put an end to all this.'

'You must bring an end to this terrible, bitter atrocity.'

'What you are is a gift. A gift from a planet that does not deserve it and that can do nothing to save itself from oblivion.'

'Listen to us. Listen.'

Random screwed his eyelids so tight that tears began to flow. Were these his parents? What gift?

'Why me?' he cried. 'Why must I be the one to stop all of this? I don't even know who I am.'

'You are born of war but we did not programme you to hate. Remember that, no matter how difficult your predicament may become.'

The boy sniffed, overwhelmed by emotion.

'I don't want to. I can't fight. I won't fight!' he spat through clenched teeth.

'You will find another way. But you must stay here. Through the power we have given to you, it is necessary. It is your destiny.'

'Screw my destiny! If this war has been raging for centuries then whose going to listen to a boy? The rest of them haven't. I won't do it.'

'You must.'

'I refuse to!'

Random shot out of his seat and belted towards the mid-section, but was stopped by the presence of Skateboard, who had propped himself up in the doorway.

Although the robot had no eyes to speak of, Random could feel the look of bewilderment directed in his path.

'Sir, I don't mean to speak out of terms.'

'Then don't,' Random sniffed and pushed his way past and into the direction of the living quarters.

Skateboard turned to face the distressed child. He had caught only a few seconds of the lad's struggle and presumed that he had been speaking to someone. In fear, he had prepared his stun gun, which protruded from his shell like a straw bobbing in a glass of fizzy drink.

Cautiously, he double checked that the room was empty and made after his new companion.

Skateboard found Random sobbing into his arms as he slumped over the desk in his quarters. Nervously, he spoke, giving an indignant cough to make the boy aware of his existence.

'How much did you hear?'

'Not much, to tell you the truth, Sir, only something about not wanting to fight, or fulfill your destiny. Did I get the jist?'

Random nodded, wiped away his tears and cleared his throat.

'I'm not like the others, Skateboard. In truth, I think I'm only a few days old. I woke up in a chamber, a glass chamber, and all I could see around me was death and destruction.

There were a couple of dead bodies in the room; I think it was some kind of scientist's office, one was blue, and the other was red.

I didn't check to see if they were alive. There was a craft there too, like the ones that attacked us. It had crashed.

There was fire, so much smoke and I did what only I could. I ran. I kept running, until I got caught by some soldiers from the Crimson Empire. I managed to escape but I am so confused. Why me? I don't feel ready.'

Random sat cross legged on the ground and ran his right hand over Skateboard reassuringly.

'I don't look like everyone else either, my friend. I seem to be a mixture of both these sides.'

'What do you mean?' enquired Skateboard.

'Look at me.'

And so Skateboard did. He adjusted his optical senses and gazed his in-built lenses on the boy sat at his side.

Random could hear a faint whirring of inner motors as the AI took in the revelation. After a few moments, he stopped.

'I don't want to sound ignorant, Sir, but what about it?'

Random scoffed.

'Well, let's just say that I'm not going to pass as either a member of the Crimson Empire or the Sapphire Regime.'

'It doesn't make a difference, Sir. In my circuits, you are indeed a gift. So what if you were created in a laboratory. As I get to know you, it might even explain a few things!'

The boy chuckled; he was relieved that this little robot had been developed with a sense of humour.

'What's more; you're the first person who has treated me like an equal since I have been created. I could spend an eternity searching my memory banks for another like you but I can't find one. So yes, you are unique, but that doesn't mean it's a bad thing. If you need help, then I am here to help you. If you want to stay and fight, then I'll stay by your side, but if you truly wish to escape, then have a serious think first and maybe clear your head in a different part of the galaxy for a while.'

Random wiped his nose with his sleeve and smiled.

'You mean that?'

'Why not? This war isn't going anywhere. It'll still be here when you get back.'

'But what about the innocent? When I was running away I came across a baron wasteland. There were literally dozens of people; men, women, children. I couldn't look in their eyes. I couldn't look at any of them. I felt shame.'

'There was nothing to feel shameful about. You hadn't done anything to put those people there.'

'But I've got these voices in my head telling me I can save them.' Random started to cry again. He proceeded to pull his sleeve up to his dripping nose. Skateboard was appalled by his friend's lack of manner and shot out a thin, robotic arm from his back that came complete with a white handkerchief and held it up to his master's nose. Random sniffed and then blew into the handkerchief and when he was done, the robot tied it up with the same claw and flung it straight into the waste bin at the side of the desk. Random was impressed for a second, and then he went back to concentrating on his inner confliction.

'I think that if you are the one to put an end to this, you need to be sure in your mind what to do. Right now, you are not. Yes, there is a crisis on Rodas, but then again, Sir, there is a crisis on every plain in the cosmos. There is unnecessary suffering in every corner of existence. It is the way of the universe. But there are some that can triumph over that suffering and although it might never put an end to it completely, if just one person's life is saved, then you will learn to feel good in what you have done. But, and I'm being as frank as a series-two artificial intelligence robot can be, I don't think that this is your time to have a say in that suffering.
You have a long future ahead of you, I am sure of it, and when the time is right, you will come back here and you will save those people in the wastelands. If you're right about this "destiny" to save Rodas, then you will leave this planet in its redemption before your time is at an end. But today is not that day, nor tomorrow. One day in the future you'll be back, I'm sure of it. But for now, your immediate destiny is away from here. So what's to say we get out of here for now and leave the future to the days to come?'

Random's tears were quickly evaporating. Spurred on by his metallic friend's speech, he hugged the robot and smiled.

'Thank you.'

'Never a problem, Sir, although I might have to charge you next time,' Skateboard joked.

Random got to his feet and made for the doorway back into the mid-section with Skateboard following close behind. There was a new bond between the two. Random, for the first time in his life, had a friend and likewise for Skateboard. His words had made Random feel a thousand times better than he had and the cherry on the top was that the voices had, for now at least, disappeared.

Random had a sense of purpose.
Of course he was not ready to take on an army by himself, although a feeling inside him told him he could. A spirit had awoken. He was beginning to understand who he was now. Yes, he could become the saviour of Rodas, but not today.

Today was about saving himself.

XIV

In the relative safety of the operations bay, Everald sat pensive, his fingers tapping against the corners of his mouth, deep in a thoughtful trance. He had failed. The Crimson Empire had been ordered by his Master to engage with the purple child and eliminate him. But there was no sight of the boy anywhere on Rodas. The waste fields, sand dunes and crumbling cities were investigated with a fine tooth comb and there was no evidence that he had been there. And now, the news had just got worse.

Soldiers on the front line outside the Sapphire Regime's Headquarters reported just clicks ago that a prototype fighter craft had been spotted engaging both the Red and Blue factions, however before either side had the chance to claim victory over who could put an end to both warring sides, he had defeated them.

How?

By applying the brakes on his ship and letting the others crash into one another. The casualties for both the allies and their enemies had been appalling and yet nobody lost their lives. It was the fighters involved that would never see the light of day again as they were now nothing but scrap metal.

Everald was met with the terrifying thought of a) having to explain his men's futile attempts to capture and kill the perpetrator to his Master and b) trying to cover up the fact that 200 heli-fighters were now out of commission from the auditors who were visiting the following morning. Everald shivered in his chair. He couldn't decide which predicament was more alarming!

He broke from his concentration and noticed that the Operations Bay was now empty. It was just he, alone, in the whole control room. He couldn't use his office since he destroyed it in a fit of rage and now he was where he never wanted to be; by himself.

'My, my, my,' said a chilling voice from the shadows. 'You have no control over your temper, do you Everald.'

The Sergeant shot up from his seat, gave the customary salute of two fingers in both his ears to his Master and attempted to find an excuse for his actions.

'I had to get rid of them all, Sir. They were insolent.'

'As are you, my friend.' The red-hooded figure stayed in the gloom of the shadows, although there was not much light left to give in the operations bay as Everald had ironically blown the fuse box when his internal fuse gave out.

'Where are they all now?'

'I dismissed them all and sent them to the salt mines for two weeks. It's the least I could do.'

'No, I don't believe that somehow. The least that you could have done was to band your troops together as a unit and give me what I wanted; an end to the child of Rodas.'

Everald gulped.

'Master, he will be found. I swear on my Mother's life.'

'You don't have a Mother, Everald. You're a clone, remember?'

'Sorry, it's a term I once heard one of my men use.'

The voice grew louder in volume but stayed soft in its tone.

'You are incompetent, aren't you? When I promoted you to this role, I saw great promise. Unfortunately you've left me with nothing but disappointment. I left you to watch over my army as I planned an end to all things. Now I confess, I made a mistake. Who was watching the watcher?'

'Master, please. Spare me. Give me another chance to prove my worthiness to yourself and the Crimson Empire's cause. With your support, I can help us ascend to glory.'

'You know the picture has always been bigger than just Rodas, Everald.

When the blue pestilence has been exterminated, we can then grow across Ursa-17. Ascend to the outer reaches of the galaxy and spread our influence across the peoples of the universe. For that, I need the best by my side; the very best.'

Everald was silent. His pupils shrank and his throat went dry as the sweat began to pour. Blood red droplets began to seep from his pores. He knew what was coming next.

'And you are not the very best, are you?' Everald's spirit died inside. He wasn't the least bit concerned for anything else now, other than his own wellbeing. And like the shallow creature that he was, he knew that not even appealing to his Master's better side could save his skin.

'In here, there is a whole army of soldiers who are better than you. They have been here all along, right under your nose and you never even noticed.'

'Do you mean my men?'

'No, Everald. Your men are pithy. They have fought too many campaigns. No more do they carry the scars of war than the scars of war carry them.

'At the end of the day, you are all damaged goods. I need a new army and very soon, I'll have one. Void of the horror of fight after fight.
I've been building them for some time and yet all it took was just a little bit of the best traits from

my warriors, cherry picking attributes from soldier to soldier to create them. Why, I even extracted from you and you didn't feel a thing.'

The quivering Sergeant stood aghast at the coming revelations.

'You've been cloning the Crimson Empire?'

'Hmm.' The hooded figure moved in the shadows, edging just a little closer to his terrified mind.

'Not just cloning from us but cloning from them as well. The salt mines and concentration camps make for such glorious specimens. This is a process that has been going on since before you were born.'

'But we hate the Sapphire Regime.'

'Why? Why do we hate them?

Everald searched his memory. Incredible. He didn't really know the answer. Nobody did. The civil war had raged for so long that generations of families had grown up knowing only one thing - to hate those unlike them.

'Rodas is dying and we are the disease. We need a clean slate. I shall lead us to glory…not you. No longer in the shadows – but leading from the front.'

'But we've never had that kind of technology. Neither have they. Reconnaissance has never indicated that the Sapphire Regime has the capability to clone.'

'That's because my soldiers were ordered to keep things from ever going public. So private were the reports that not even you were made aware of them. But we both had the capabilities. Indeed, this child was created using stolen elements from our technology but as he is unsullied, he must be purged.'

'Then Master, I beg of you,' Everald pleaded, 'Now that you have told me your plans, let me be the one who finds him and puts an end to all of this.'

'I don't want to put an end to anything, my servant. A full stop will not be made on the fighting, it'll go on, but it'll leave the confines of this planet and spawn until I have total power. Only the life of the boy will cease. With my new army in place, not even he will be able to hide forever. There are many who will not live to see this new world.'

He turned and stared blankly into the eyes of the quivering wreck that stood before him.

'Including you, Everald.'

'Master…' a tear squeezed out of the corner of his eye and trickled down his cheek. The Master gazed down on his subject, calm and subdued, but nonetheless powerful. The Master raised his voice all the time to those below Everald's ranking. He had always possessed a soft spot for his obedient servant. But it was when he said nothing at all, that the hearts of all living beings understood their fate.

'Kneel.'

'I can be by your side. I can help you ascend into glory!'

'Kneel.'

'I…I…I can rectify my failings in your guidance, Sir.'

'Kneel.'

'I'll do anything you say, Master. Anything. I'll tear down our army. Rebuild it again in your image. I am your one, true servant!' Everald panicked, his breath heavy with the knowing that his life was about to end.

'If you were my one true servant, you'd be kneeling for me now.'

Sniveling like a schoolboy who had just been mugged of his dinner money, Everald sank to his knees.

'Oh, Everald. I had such high hopes for you. Still, I'll have better luck next time.'

With one fell swoop, the Master stepped forward from the shadows. His features were no longer obscured by the darkness. Everald gazed in utter terror at the face of his executioner.

After one laboured final breath, his life force was torn from his chest as his heart was ripped clean from its housing inside his ribcage. Bereft of life, his dead eyes stared into the very soul of death himself. And death, with the heart of the slain in his hand, starred back.

XV

The moment of reckoning had arrived. Under the cover of broad daylight, the Venus II was to make its ascent on the security mainframe and break free of Rodas. It would be a momentous moment for the planet as a glimmer of hope would be delivered freakishly by accident in the act of escape and in doing so, Random and Skateboard would become the first sentient beings since the governments of Ursa-17, 18 and 19 had contained the war centuries earlier.

'Right, 76 clicks and we'll be close to the barrier. Skateboard, do you have the countdown? We don't want to hit anything other than on the count of 40 clicks otherwise we'll be fried.'

In the few days since his impossible inception, Random had already grown more authoritative over Skateboard. Not that the AI cared. As long as he was treated fairly, like any service robot would like to be treated, they'd continue to get along nicely. In his circuitry, he knew that it was best to let him find his feet and confidence in his own way, especially as he knew deep down in his memory wafers that this child was special.

'Reading you loud and clear, Captain.'

'Captain? Okay, Captain it is then.

Thanks...err...Commander.' Random said;

pleased at the reputation he appeared to have with Skateboard.

'I'm honoured Sir, but here on Rodas, there's a law against making those of artificial intelligence - robots, if you will - a person of rank. Ever since the great disaster that was General Sinsapol.'

'Really? What did he do?'

'He had a screw lose.'

Random stared confused, and then grasped what his friend had said. He possessed super strength and the capacity to do amazing things and yet Random could be a little slow on the uptake.

'Well, we won't be on Rodas much longer and then you can be my Commander. I promise,' smiled Random.

'Thank you, Sir.' Skateboard's electro-mechanical workings whirred in excitement. 'And now, back to the task in hand, don't you think. This won't be easy.'

'What are you talking about? Of course it will be. Just make sure we make it through on the 40th click and whoosh, we're away!'

'I believe you might be forgetting something, Captain. You're a wanted man. I mean boy. I feel I may have to remind you that you not only have the most powerful army on this planet looking for you but you also have the second most powerful army on your back. The cloaking device has worked so far but we have to switch it off to guarantee ourselves enough power to break through the mainframe.'

Random sighed audibly and rolled his eyes.

'Oh yeah. Well, we'd better be quick then. How many clicks now?'

'47 until we reach our destination,' informed Skateboard.

'And that's half the journey, knowing the destination.'

'Very profound, Sir. It's time to open engines three and four.'

Random leant to his right, keeping his eyes ahead of him and flicked the switch that opened up all four engine bays.

As soon as he did, the sound of his action roared furiously within the bowels of the ship. When the duo were carrying out the repairs and upgrades, they had discovered that the Venus had untapped potential when it came to speed, velocity and power.

So when they fell upon the Venus's capacity for double the capacity for light speed with the flick of a switch, they realised that they had the potential to outrun any heli-fighter - if they were not discovered first.

'Right, starting our climb…now!' Random pulled the steering column up and the ship's nose changed from a horizontal to a near-vertical position. The Venus subsequently tore its way through the sky and shot towards the sky.

'Wait a second,' said Random. 'I can't see any security barrier. Where the heck is it? Is it cloaked like us?'

'No, Sir, it is protected by a perception filter. When people look up at the sky they see the stars. It's an illusion. I probably should have warned you before. I hope it doesn't cause you any distress.'

'Distress? Thanks!' Random said. He had initially been under the impression that they had planned this escape to every detail. Clearly not!

'No more surprises, okay, my metal friend?'

'Understood, Captain,' confirmed Skateboard.

His hands vibrated on the steering wheel as the Venus continued to climb.

'10 clicks to the barrier.'

Random kept his eyes on the stars in front of him as Skateboard continued to count down. With every click, the engines roared louder and the Venus shuddered under the continued force that was crushing down upon it.

'4…3…2…1'

With the blink of an eye, the stars fell out of existence.

'Return us to horizontal flight,' Skateboard instructed.

Random was stunned by what he saw. For as far as his eyes could see, there was a metal mesh covering the entire outer atmosphere of Rodas. Knitted together in a cold grasp, keeping the planet contained. Random squinted and made out little command centres, each one manned by beings that were neither red nor blue in complexion. Nor were they purple!

Random gulped.

'I didn't realise there'd be people out here. I thought this mainframe would just be, you know, self-powered or something.'

'It is,' explained Skateboard. 'But the people of our neighbouring galaxies could not afford anybody to get out.'

'Why not?'

'Well, you've seen the devastation the people of Rodas have caused. Can you imagine that out there among the stars?'

'Didn't these so-called governments think it would be a better idea to try and put a stop to it instead of leave people here to die?'

'Sadly not; they decided that at the end of the day, it wasn't really their problem.' Skateboard could feel a sense of injustice bubbling under Random's surface. His brow furrowed, his lips pursed and his eyes narrowed.

'No one should ever have quarantined Rodas. Not if they'd seen what I've seen,' he said.

'Maybe they knew something that we didn't,' suggested Skateboard.

In an instance a massive power surge boomed around the ship, rocking it so hard that the elastic snapped on the furry dice that dangled on the top dashboard.

'Here comes the power surge, Sir. I suggest we observe this one and wait for the next,' advised Skateboard.

Random dug his nails into the arm rests of his chair and felt the pulse shoot through the mainframe like a wave of electricity. The crash of thunder echoed all around them and the blast of energy split Random's ear drums to such an extent that they continued to ring for a couple of minutes afterwards.

A shock of blue shot through the mainframe and left in an instant, leaving the barrier momentarily down for no longer than five seconds before it powered up again.

'So, what causes this pulse?' asked Random.

'It's the regenerative power that it works off. Every 40 clicks it needs to momentarily power down before it sparks up again to shock the whole system back into life. The reason being is because the replacement power kicks in when the old power source is down and charging up again. Does that explain it, Sir?'

Random nodded. 'Absolutely,' he lied.

A second roar of engines replaced the crackle of energy. Only this time, the engines sounded more powerful than ever before.

'Skateboard, have the engines gone into overdrive?'

'No, Sir; at least, I don't think so. I'll run a diagnostic now.' Skateboard's circuits whizzed into life as the noise grew louder.

'It doesn't sound like our engines. It sounds like a whole army of…oh…'

Random dared not finish his sentence. He looked out of the front window and stared in utter astonishment as the Crimson Empire fleet slowly rose through the perception filter. It wasn't just any fleet. This was a full armada.

The boy trembled in fear, reaching down with his right hand to pat Skateboard for his own assurance.

'Say there, my old pal. Is the cloaking device still on?'

'Yes, Sir.'

'So they can't see us right?'

'Right.'

'Not quite, I'm afraid my boy.'

A new voice boomed through the speakers. It made Random's skin shiver. It was so calm, a sinister tint to the tones made his intent clear.

Random knew that they were in serious trouble now.

'We can't see you but we know that you are out there.'

Skateboard pulled himself into the corner of the cockpit.

'I know that voice,' he shuddered.

'You thought that you could get away from me, did you boy? I admire your courage and guile. It's taken us a long time to find you and yet here you are.'

Random gulped. 'Turn the communication channels on, Skateboard.'

'But Sir –'

'Just do it!'

Skateboard dragged his metallic frame over to the dashboard and opened the communications.

'Yeah, but you can't see me, can you? In fact, you have absolutely no idea where I am. I could be behind you or right in front of your nose.'

'Ah,' the voice echoed in delight. 'You are trying to play a little game with me, are you boy? Hide and seek. If that is your wish, we have got

plenty of time. I'll find you eventually. Even if I have to wait forever, I'll take you to task and I'll locate you in the end.'

The boy sweated profusely.

'Who are you?'

'It is not of any importance.'

'It is to me. I want to know who you are, what you are and why you want me dead.'

The speakers fell silent. The Venus II shuddered as another bolt shot through the mainframe. They had missed their first window. Meanwhile, the beings inside the command centre of the main frame stood aghast at the appearance of the Crimson armada - unable to act. If any force were to be used, the security ships of Ursa 16 through to 19 would have to be notified - for the good of the galaxy.

'My name is Kalor Maloso. I am the ruler of the Crimson Empire. Why do I want to put an end to your troubling existence? Well, let's just say that you do not fit in my plans but you could severely damage them.'

Random let out an impromptu chuckle.

'So that's why you want me dead? I "don't fit in with your plans"? Rubbish!
You'll have to do better than that! I could be the most insignificant being in the whole of the cosmos as far as you were concerned.'

'It has not escaped our attention that your conception was more than a little…unconventional. You're an unstable element in the game of war on this planet.'

'I think you're the unstable one here, mate! I'm not the one killing millions of innocent people!'

'No, but you could be.'

Random slumped back in his chair, feeling slightly exhausted by the whole exchange so far.

'So war's just a game to you, is it? D'you know what, Maloso? I'm beginning to see the full picture here. I'm not the unstable element here. You are!'

'I'd advise you not to try my temper, boy.' Maloso spat. He did not raise his voice but there was a growing intensity in his words.

'Sir, please. I beg of you. Don't take him to task. He is dangerous. Evil! We can find another port along the mainframe if we switch to silent running. That way they won't pick our engines up on their heat trackers,' whispered Skateboard.

There was a sense of enormous panic in Skateboard's voice. It made Random ponder the almighty task in front of him. If this man, this Kalo Maloso, was bad enough to make an AI frightened, how dangerous must he really be?

'I'll tell you what, Maloso. I don't think you are as high and mighty as you and your armada are making yourselves out to be.

You see the great lengths you've gone too to try and stop just one boy? You've driven your entire fleet to the very edge of Rodas itself just to stop me. And do you know why? It's because you're afraid, isn't it? That's the reason why you want to stop me. You're scared of me.'

'Do not try my patience, boy; I have slaughtered many who have used words of insolence such as you are now.'

'Then why don't you come and find me? Come on, what's stopping you?'

Maloso's tones began to strain under the increasing pressure that Random was putting him under. Unbeknownst to our hero - sorry, idiot - was that he was making the head of the Crimson Empire look stupid in front of his armada.

'Oh yes, of course. We're cloaked. So what else have you got, Maloso?'

Before Random could continue, a terrifying wall of laser fire shot like beacons of death from the armada and fizzed with great speed towards the Venus. Random took evasive action and plunged towards the steering column and took his vessel into a nose dive that kept it safe from the firepower. He looked up out of the viewer and saw the sea of death, the span of the vast armada itself wash over the Venus.

He breathed a sigh of relief before another barrage spurted from the warships; this time on another level closer to the vessel's hiding spot.

'We'll keep firing until we hit you and your pathetic excuse of a craft.'

Maloso was no longer playing for time. Random had failed. He really was going to die. The Venus shuddered from yet another jolt of energy and the mainframe indicated a further missed opportunity for escape.

'Skateboard, any ideas?' Random expression of concern appeared like it was on the verge of descending into full on panic.

Another sea of laser fire shot towards the Venus II and Random had to nose dive away from the threat again.

'None, I'm afraid, Sir. It looks like he is forcing us away from the mainframe. I think he knows what we are planning to do.'

'Shavzit!' Random swore.

'Alright, Maloso, you've made your point. We'll come quietly.'

'Oh no, I don't want you to surrender, my boy. I want the pleasure of ending your existence right here, right now. I could hunt you all day and night. It'll make the act of killing you all the more pleasant.'

Before another wave of lasers emitted from the armada, there was yet another rumble of energy; but it wasn't from the mainframe or Maloso's ships. There was another army penetrating the skies of Rodas. Only this time, Random did not recognize the ships. There were just as many ships as those from the Crimson Empire and they were just as dark and foreboding as those that he had faced before. Skateboard's circuits whirred in astonishment. The controllers in the security mainframe began to panic. The biggest fleet stand-off was about to take place above the skies of Rodas and although security was on its way, there could be no guarantee that they would be able to stop them – whatever they planned to do next.

'We're doomed.'

Random frowned. 'What, more doomed than we already are?'

'I'm afraid so, Sir. This is the main battle fleet of the Sapphire Regime. I recognize the ships. You see that one on the far left?'

'What? The one that looks like a giant nose?'

'The Nostrildamus, yes, that's the one. That was my first commission.'

'Well, as much as I'd like to sit here and flick through the pages of your autobiography, Skateboard, what the flip do we do now!'

Skateboard indignantly turned to his friend.

'We die.'

XVI

'Kalor Maloso. You are in direct violation of this air space.'

A new voice, equally as calm and yet more in control than that of the ruby dictator, oozed over the speakers in the Venus II.

'What is your reasoning behind this trespassing? You know that our agreement forbids us to intercept this section of the planet.'

Random looked at Skateboard and was about to ask who this new voice belonged to, however he did not need to as Maloso unknowingly answered his query.

'Gres Masmun. This is an unexpected surprise. I wouldn't go as far as saying that it is a pleasure to hear your voice again.'

Random looked at Skateboard with a puzzled look amongst his face.

'As High Chancellor of the Sapphire Regime I urge you to stand down. You are in violation of the Ursa treaty. If you will comply then no punishment will be given. If you do not, then we will use force.'

Maloso chuckled. 'Chancellor, you are not strong enough to put an end to me or my army. You are on the cusp of defeat in this war and now you are standing in my way in more ways than you could possibly know.'

'Yes, we are well aware of your pursuit of the purple one. Indeed, we have desires of capturing the boy ourselves for questioning.'

'Well, that's where we differ. You plan to dither whilst I plan to resolve his threat once and for all.'

'They do tend to talk a bit too much, don't you think?' Random whispered to his robotic friend.

'Megalomaniacs are all the same, I'm afraid. They all like the sounds of their voices too much,' he replied.

Yet another bolt of energy fizzed through the mainframe and another glimmer of escape evaporated. Fortunately Random had a plan.

'What if we take advantage of this and sneak off while they are talking.'

Skateboard whirred in thought. 'A good idea, Captain, but we risk flying into the laser fire if they decide to attack. We'd be caught in the crossfire and blasted out of the sky!'

'Well, let's make sure we go as soon as possible then. How far away are we?'

'We are further away now – around 83 semi-clicks. I suggest we use silent running so they don't track the heat from our engine then decloak and use our light speed capabilities before either fleets have a chance to fire on us.'

'Well, don't just sit there, let's do it!' Random flew into his chair, strapped himself in and pulled the steering column towards his body as the Venus II crawled, click by click, tentatively back towards the main frame. All the while, both Maloso and Masmun had continued with their war of words.

'...well, if you weren't so scared of attacking our main HQ then we wouldn't think that you were as insipid in your efforts as you are in your insults.'

'We don't have time for this' replied Maloso, 'I'll give you three clicks to move aside or we shall blow you out of the sky.'

'Sir...,' said Skateboard.

'One...'

'I know, Skateboard. Hold onto something.' Random advised.

'Two...'

'I can't. I don't have arms.'

'Three!'

Random put his foot down on the accelerator pedal and shot at velocity towards the mainframe.

'FIRE!' Maloso screamed.

'RETURN FIRE!' Masmun retorted.

Random clenched his buttocks so hard he nearly split his trousers. The Venus II, at top speed, was vertically ascending towards a metal wall that had not been penetrated ever before. It was surging towards a barrage of red laser fire from the right and blue laser fire from the left. Two walls of death and fatality flooded towards the vessel above them, about to crash together with devastating force.

The two barriers of light were gaining, sliding together like doors closing in front of them.

'Five clicks to the next pulse' Skateboard panted; if he had pores, he would have been situated in a puddle of sweat by now.

'How many clicks are we away from the mainframe?'

'About 10 clicks.'

'I'm going to do it.' Random took off the cloak. The Venus was spotted by Maloso. From the bridge of his command freighter he hollered intensely at the sight of his prey.

'There he is! Fire, shoot on him now! DESTROY HIM!'

FOUR

'Don't,' Skateboard panicked.

THREE

'I must!' Random felt for the light speed lever.

TWO

'Sir, we won't – '

'ONE'

'Here we go!'

Random pressed the lever down and the Venus II disappeared totally from sight. It had slotted through the mainframe at just the right moment. The pulse had powered down and the Venus II had slipped through the eye of a needle.

The bolts of laser fire from both fleets had left the narrowest of gaps for the vessel to escape. A click later, the energy that powered the mainframe ebbed away, leaving the metal net vulnerable for puncture from a small ship. Just a few clicks below, the red and blue laser fire collided like positive and negative energy and created the most beautiful horizon of brilliant purple that the entire cosmos had ever seen.

The shock of purple stained the skies as the impact of energy sent both armadas reeling like giant hawks of death caught in a hurricane. Maloso fell to the ground, as did the rest of his men, banging his head in the process; luckily, he was able to look up and see the brilliant wonder of the image before him before he fell to the ground.

Far below, on the ravaged plains of Rodas, the refugees of the worst war in the history of the cosmos stared disbelievingly into the night sky.

Stretching wide across the plain, the casualties and outcasts of both the Crimson and Sapphire factions of the decimated, ruined planet looked up and saw the sight that no one in the chronicles of this shunned sector of Ursa-17 had ever barred witness to before.

Many cried in wonderment and others bore smiles that had never spread across their lips in their entire, miserable lives. Women and children stood hand-in-hand looking up to the sky in total silence at a colour they had never seen before. It was the colour that had started the seemingly futile conflict in the first place.

Purple. Brilliant, vibrant purple.

A feeling began to pulsate through the sick, the captured, the defeated and the stricken that rejuvenated their lives in a way that nothing had ever done before.

With the explosion of one simple colour in the sky, Random had inadvertently done it.

The idiot, so intent on running away from his purpose, had disappeared without a trace and in his wake, he had left a message; a feeling that had the potential to revolutionise a planet as troubled as Rodas.

Hope.

XVII

All the while, the Venus had managed to negotiate its way through the main frame and had left Rodas, Maloso, the Crimson Empire, the Sapphire Regime and - he hoped - the Sandman - in its dust.

'Woo hoo! We've done it! I can't believe it!' Random punched the air repeatedly in triumph. They had escaped the planet that no-one had ever attempted or even dared to dream breaking free from. As the Venus II had pierced the main frame netting, he had been blissfully unaware of the events happening below.

'Skateboard, we've done it! Skateboard?' Random glanced all around the cockpit and could see no sight of his robotic companion. There was a trail of crude oil that started in the space that the AI had occupied. It led right underneath the co-pilots chair and it was there that Random saw Skateboard, quivering like jelly, his hydraulics squeaking involuntarily.

'Er…sorry, Captain. I profess that I never doubted your plan for a second.'

Random hummed indignantly. 'Don't worry, my friend. I won't tell anyone.'

'About what?'

'The puddle.'

Skateboard looked quizzically and then shot across the cockpit, smearing the oil into the floor.

'My apologies, Sir.' If robots could blush, Skateboard's complexion would have been redder than the entire Crimson Empire. 'I'll clean it up right away.'

'Why bother, let's celebrate!' Random flicked the button labeled AUTO-PILOT and vacated his chair. An imprint of nervous sweat was left on the back of the seat.

'I must admit, it was closer than I expected.'

He walked out of the cockpit into the mid-section and proceeded to raid the cupboards for a drink. He found a bottle of unbranded liquid and casually discarded the screw top and swigged the whole thing back before belching like a walrus after 100 gallons of fizzy drink.

Skateboard joined him in the kitchen.

'Beg your pardon, Captain…quite literally, but where would you like to go?'

Random threw the bottle to one side and plonked himself down in a nearby chair.

'Do you know what? I have no idea. I mean, what's out there except Rodas?'

'Well, in my down time I used to study star charts and our historical archives from before the war took full effect.

The people of Rodas were once profound explorers; clever scholars who would sail the systems charting new worlds, inspiring the people at home. When I would digitally peruse the archives, I discovered a multitude of nebulas in the vicinity. There are so many places to discover that sound utterly delightful. There's the twelve planets of the Obligas system, where three of them have no western hemisphere due to a blueprint error on behalf of the planet engineers commissioned to work on the Obligas extension.'

'No. I don't think so. What else?'

'Let me see. There's a planet in the Tragonium arm of Ursa-9 where they say it rained food.

'What? How?'

'The ecosystem allows for the combative bombardment of food particles to collect in clouds where their molecules are reconstructed to its precise original taste and look. It was a revolutionary method that ended up putting an end to famine on Tragonia.'

Random licked his lips. 'That does sound tempting. It's a bit close to home though isn't it? I mean, Ursa-9 is only…' he counted on his digits, '…eight Ursa's away from our current location.'

Skateboard hesitated.

'What now?' Random said.

'We forgot to take the auto-pilot off, didn't we?'

Random's naturally purple complexion went white. He leapt from the comfort of his chair, sped into the cockpit and slumped back into the wet, sweaty chair.

'Cribes!' he exclaimed.

He slapped the auto-pilot off in a hurry. A fantastic blur of stars spiraling by slowly ebbed away. The beautiful sight of light speed was soon replaced by the giant vision of a huge planet, swamping the view screen.

'Turn right!' Skateboard shrieked as he connected with the Venus and attempted to curb the speed of the craft even further.

The Venus II continued to slow but the picture of the blue/green planet in front of them was growing ever seismic.

'I can't hold it, Skateboard!' Random's hands were shuddering so hard against the sheer velocity of the ship's descent that it made the steering column shake violently; so vigorously that Random's slim cheeks were bouncing so hard that it was making the rest of his features vibrate and blur like a painting melting in the heat.

'Put your foot down all the way on the break.'

'Oh, yes, why didn't I think of that? I thought I'd put it down on the accelerator,' said Random sarcastically. 'What an idiot I am!'

'No time for sarcasm, Sir. We've entered the atmosphere now. Suggest crash landing maneuvers.'

'You never taught me that, Skateboard.' Skateboard's audio circuits had trouble ciphering what Random had said as the Captain was shaking so much now.

The Venus was still growing in velocity as the gravitational pull dragged it closer to a fiery end. Random could make out what looked like a blue ocean below a thin layer of cloud, which the Venus pierced with the grace of a moose falling through a giant piece of paper 40 miles above ground. Random finally managed to pull the ship up, just clicks before it slammed into the cold sea. He managed to bring the ship to horizontal flight and skillfully only just avoided what appeared to Random and Skateboard as very striking and dangerous white cliffs.

'I'm going to try to land this thing safely somewhere,' he barked, no longer being thrown around like a child on a bouncy castle.

However, the ship was still coming in too fast and as the Venus II cleared what looked like a settlement of civilization, Random slammed the breaks on so hard that the nose section of the vessel dug itself in the soft ground, rendering the boy instantly unconscious as the whole craft began pin-wheeling several times across a vibrant field, crashing through a collection of centuries old trees and eventually grinding to a halt on the edge of a lake, upside down.

The echoes of fallen foliage rang around the forest and the chirps and squeals of alarmed wildlife rang true all around. When the dust and the noise settled down, the landing gear shot out to the blue sky with almost comedic timing.

The only beings around to witness the terrible crash were two schoolchildren; both were stood aghast at the edge of the other side of the lake.

Little did they know now but when Random and Skateboard would finally come to, they'd soon realise that they had crash landed on the only planet that could compare with the atrocities committed by the world they had broken free from.

Earth.

CHAPTER TWO

BEGINNINGS

I

Anji Gummadi had always had a taste for adventure. At the tender age of two she wandered away from her parents on a shopping trip in the Brunswick Centre and ventured onto a red bus unnoticed and ended up at St Paul's Cathedral. Her panic-stricken parents were relieved to find her but what bemused them most about their only child's impromptu journey was that a toddler with no idea of the dangers of the world had somehow managed to negotiate the London transport system and somewhere in her journey, must have changed buses to reach her destination!

Anji had always been a little different from her peers – even at an early age. Her Mother and Father had settled upon England's capital on a whim. Nothing more than a spur-of-the-moment decision, initiated by her Father, Krishnan, upon hearing that his new wife, Myra, was carrying his baby so that they could give their unborn child a better chance at life than he could provide in Rajasthan – one of the poorest areas in India.

So, with the news of an impending arrival in the Gummadi household, Krishnan and Myra scrapped together what little money they had, filled out all the necessary visa application forms and sailed among the clouds to a whole new world.

Despite their uneducated background, the Gummadi's found jobs rather quickly. Krishnan worked as a porter in a North London hospital whilst Myra found employment as a dinner lady not far from her husband. They settled into a rented two-bedroom flat just outside of Tottenham and when Anji was born, they had everything and more than they could ever have wished for.

Sadly, their happiness didn't last long. One sizzling summer's day, whilst Anji was at nursery school, her parents were the victims of a car accident which left the little girl alone, homeless and an orphan. Tragically, they had been on their way to pick up their smiley three-year-old to take her for an afternoon out at London Zoo – a place that Anji had dreamed about visiting ever since she'd seen a poster advertising it on the London Underground.

From that moment on, the little girl's life was turned upside down. From a life of reasonable comfort and security, she spent the next nine years of her life bounding from children's home to children's home, school to school, desperately seeking an escape. To what? She didn't know.

Even a spell at an all-girl's boarding school in Essex didn't stop young Anji from running away.

Potential foster parents came and went whilst her behaviour bordered from disruptive to destructive. From petty crime, such as stealing sweets from local newsagents to setting fire to PE kits at school, Anji was beginning to gain a reputation as a tear-away, with good reason!

She wanted to find something to fill the vast hole her parent's deaths had left.

At the age of 11, she felt like she was starting to reach a turning point in her life. She had settled in St Bernard's Children's Home, joined a local comprehensive where some of her fellow orphans attended and even put an end to her destructive ways. Upon reflection, as she entered her teenage days, she put her time setting fire to her classmate's shorts and thieving food and magazines from Benson's corner shop down as 'a passing phase.'

She had even grown fond of her carers at the home and for the first time, she was starting to look up to them as role models. But her spirit for adventure still burned bright.

'Come on, Anji. Get off that phone! You're missing everything!'

Miss Carter, Anji's Geography teacher, had taken class 3B on a field trip to Dartmoor National Park in a bid to get the lead air of the city out of her student's lungs and try to give them an inspirational view of country life. Yet, so far, her efforts had been in vain.

'If I catch anyone else texting or playing on your phone then I'm afraid I'll have to take them off of you all and lock them away in the bus.'

A chorus of moans and groans rang around the boys and girls of 3B and they all proceeded to put their mobile devices back in their pockets and bags.

'Ah-ha-ha. Turn them off, not on silent. I wasn't born yesterday.' She hollered as she led the line of teenagers across a boggy field.

'Shame - could have started your personality from scratch,' whispered Jake, the blonde haired, squeaky voiced class clown.

'I heard that, Jake!' Miss Carter replied. 'One more word out of you and you'll be sitting next to me on the coach back!'

Jake's heart skipped a beat and he felt his face glow red with embarrassment. Some of the children laughed and pointed at him.

'That wasn't very nice, Jake,' Anji remarked.

'I saw it in *Blackadder* the other night; thought it was quite funny.'

'What's *Blackadder*?' Anji asked. She walked beside her friend as her shoes continued to slip off her feet, getting stuck in the sticky mud.

'Can't we stick to the path, Miss? My shoes keep falling off.'

'We are on the path,' insisted Miss Carter, who could feel her ponytail becoming lose as her thick, black fringe started to straggle around her eyelids.

'Heavy rain shower last night has turned the ground to treacle. Don't worry though, we'll be in the forest soon enough.'

Anji turned around to see two of her classmates holding hands. Longingly, she looked to Jake and put her arm through his.

'Anj…what are you doing?'

'I could use a little support.'

Jake tutted, 'I can't believe you didn't bring boots with you.'

'We didn't have any spares left, did we? Unless you're talking about the left boot that was size 11 and the right that was a 7?'

'Well, I always thought you were a little imbalanced!'

Anji punched Jake's arm and chuckled. Jake always knew how to break her out of any mood. He had arrived at St Bernard's six months after Anji and over the past year, they had both developed a tight friendship.

Despite his outwardly sunny disposition, Jake's story was just as tragic as Anji's.

He was an only child and the product of a separated marriage. After his Mother ran off with his Dad's brother, his Father descended into a deep depression, soothed by a growing dependency on alcohol and before long, he struggled to cope and eventually couldn't look after Jake anymore.

Then one night, he didn't return home. Two days later his car with his wallet on the passenger's seat, was found on the Severn Bridge. Anji felt sorry for the boy when he arrived but she soon learnt that Jake was okay with his situation. He was funny, cheeky and forever smiling.

If laughter was the thing that veiled the feelings of sadness underneath, then it was a better way of dealing with things than the methods she had adopted.

'Jake?'

'Hmm.'

'What's say we break away? Y'know, maybe slip off for a couple of hours. Miss is doing my head in. You know what she'll have us doing when we get in there?'

'She'll probably break the nets out and get us pond dipping' exclaimed Jake.

'Probably. Come on. Please?' Anji stood an inch taller than Jake but even he could see the begging expression she bore.

'Oh, okay.' Jake sighed. 'I'll give you the signal then.'

But he didn't need to.

A few minutes later, whilst class 3B slipped and slid their way along the path, the bottom of their school trousers caked in a thick layer of mud, they arrived at the opening of the woods.

'Right, pick a partner, stick with them and meet back here in half an hour's time,' said Miss Carter, glad to be having a break from her demanding students.

'Erm…how will we know when to come back?' asked Jemima Wright. Anji had a severe dislike for Jemima. She was driven to school daily by her Mum in a massive Range Rover and her Father ran a local business. Whenever Jemima opened her mouth it was like Anji experienced a genuine audible allergic reaction.

'Well, you have watches, don't you?' Miss Carter said.

'No,' class 3B said in unison.

'What? None of you?'

'No.'

Miss Carter sighed, defeated. 'Oh, alright then. You can turn your phones back on.'

Class 3B cheered and rushed into their bags whilst running off into the foliage.

'But remember to come back in half an hour! No later! Otherwise, I'm declaring you missing in action!' Miss Carter waited for the children to pass her and then slumped to the ground, reached into her purse for a pack of Lambert and Butler she had confiscated earlier and sparked up a cigarette, taking a long drag before exhaling audibly.

'Bloody kids,' she muttered.

*

The children sprinted away from their minder like an army of Spartan warriors driving head first into battle. Some of the kids whooped and cheered, others like James Butcher, who must have been the only 13-year-old in the class who was there to work and not to skive from a day of classes, found a nice quiet spot in the woods and started filling in the survey his teacher had given the class on the difference between urban and rural landscapes.

Anji and Jake broke away completely from their classmates and made for a lake that they had heard about in the National Park brochure.

'What's so special about a lake?' Jake enquired.

'I find them calming.' Anji dragged Jake along with her, pouring over the map that Miss had given to each of her students.

'What's so calming about a lake?' asked Jake.

'Lots. Still water. The animals on the riverbank.'

'A riverbank on a lake? Why is it not called a lake bank, surely that would make much more sense?'

'Don't be silly,' scolded Anji. 'I think we are almost there.'

The pair had reached the outer edge of the lake and it was just as tranquil as Anji had wished. Recently, she had found that she was growing tired of the hustle and bustle of the city.

'I think it's nice to get out of London every once in a while.'

'I don't,' sulked Jake. 'No shops, no skate parks. Just fields and trees. I mean, what makes them so special?'

'Oh Jake, you and I really are different people. What am I going to do with you?' Anji sighed.

'I'll tell you what. Take me to the Grease Monkeys when we're done here. I think I've got enough pocket money to pay for the Double Double burger!'

'Jake, that's disgusting.' Anji looked away from her companion and thought that she could make out the lake.

'We're here!'

She tore away from her friend and got her phone out of her pocket. Immediately she proceeded to take pictures of the beautiful scenery. Jake jogged after her, panting all the way.

'Bloody hell, you're quick,' he spluttered, his heart wanting to escape his chest.

'You eat too much rubbish!' Anji dismissed as she snapped away.

'You're like the Mum I used to have. She'd moan about my eating habits too. Then again, the last time I remember seeing her I think I was so little I was eating rubbers off the tips of my pencils!'

'I'll remember that, might keep you quiet!'

Jake laughed. He looked up through the trees and squinted at the light shining like shards of glass through the branches.

'Looks like the suns coming out. About time; I knew I should have worn my sunglasses.'

'You don't have any, you borrowed mine, remember?'

'Oh yeah. I think I might have lost them.'

Anji tutted. 'You're useless you. I have no idea why I like you…'

Jake's eyes widened.

'…I mean…as a friend.' Anji blushed.

'Oh. Okay.'

Jake felt a warm sensation glow through his body. For a moment, he thought it was his raging hormones causing him an embarrassing moment.

'I think I'd better sit down,' he said as he found a nearby tree stump and planted himself upon it.

'I mean…if we weren't…y'know…I mean.'

Anji took pity on her friend. 'We're friends. That's all it should be right now.' She smiled the kind of smile that could melt the hardest of icebergs.

'I know. I mean, how horrible would it be if we had to move homes?' Jake tried to rationalise his feelings.

'Anj…let's say hypothetically we are both single come prom in a couple of years' time, can I baggsie you now to come with me?'

'Jake, are you asking me to be your prom date?'

Jake's face was as red a sunburned tomato.

'Yeah.'

'In two year's time?'

'Yeah.'

'What's to say that I won't be busy that night?'

The young boy tried to think of a way he could convince her.

'I'll pay for your drinks.'

'Done.' Anji held out her hand. Jake shook it. His pale clammy hands made the girl wish that she'd brought a packet of tissues along. Indiscreetly, she dried her hand on her trouser leg, joined her future date on the stump and lent her head on his shoulder.

The pair sighed in quiet contemplation.

'You're right. This is peaceful,' said Jake.

'Let's stay here as long as we can,' suggested Anji. 'I don't want to leave; the sun, the lake, that bullfrog humping that rock over there. It's all so relaxing.'

It wasn't to remain like that. Not for long.

In the faint distance, Jake could hear the sound of a jumbo jet flying overhead. It made the distilled soundtrack even more sedating. He sighed and allowed his head to roll towards Anji's.

'Anj?'

'Yes, mate?'

'Is it just me or is that plane getting closer?'

The engine sound was growing in volume by the second. The raw power and velocity sounded enormous. The sound was becoming deafening as the duo clasped their hands over their ears protecting them from the scream of machinery crashing towards them.

'Get down!' Jake pulled Anji to the ground.

Something devastating crashed through the trees, practically destroying the lake and completely squashing the horny bullfrog and smashing the poor, helpless rock to nothing but dust.

The echo of shock rang like a bell of death around the forest. In the far distance, the screams of the schoolchildren could be heard but Jake and Anji were too shell-shocked to pick the frenzy out of the chaos they had just witnessed. The pair picked themselves up, brushed themselves down as their school clothes were now caked in mud and stared open mouthed at that impossible sight before them.

Where the pond had once been, a spaceship lay crumpled and broken in the bog, with its landing gear poking out into the bright blue sky.

'What the heck is that?' Anji cried.

Jake motioned to move closer towards the craft but Anji pulled him back.

'Don't! You don't know what's in there?'

'Come on, Anj. Where's your sense of adventure? There's no fire so I think we're safe.'

Anji huffed.

'Oh, come on then!'

She pushed past Jake and made for the other side of the river bank, tripping her way over slippery twigs and moss as she went. For all his bravado, Jake was now feeling a slight twinge of anxiety.

'Maybe we should go and find Miss.'

'No! Come on Jake, like you said; sense of adventure and all that.'

'But what if whoever, whatever, is in there is...y'know?'

'Dead?'

'Exactly. It's one of my fears remember.' Jake started to follow his companion as Anji reached ever closer to the ship. She inspected the anomaly before her. The ships' gleaming hull was now scorched. It looked as though it had crash landed on its roof and what looked like a nose section was now imbedded deeply into the rock. The ship lay incongruous with its surroundings and spelt only one thing for the most hesitant of the couple.

'It looks dangerous,' said Jake as he slipped on the embankment and his left leg fell into a muddy wet puddle.

'Well, if it was, it isn't now,' Anji replied. 'I've never seen anything like it. Maybe it's a top secret government plane?'

'What if there are aliens?'

'Don't be stupid. There's no such thing as...'

Anji's dismissal was interrupted by the sudden hiss of hydraulics. She jumped as what appeared to be a ramp started to ascend out of the wreckage towards the trees that still stood as white smoke billowed from the interior.

Anji thought she could make out what looked like a figure advancing through the shadows. Jake joined her at the mouth of the ramp and stared in disbelief as the figure drew closer. They both gasped in shock as they realised who this figure was. It was a boy - and not any boy. His skin was purple. Bright, vibrant purple. He was not of their world.

'...aliens...' Anji said.

II

'Uh...where am I?

The strange, purple boy staggered and propped himself up by the doorway, clinging onto the wall to steady himself.

'Holy crap! You're an alien!' exclaimed Jake.

'A what?' the boy enquired, cupping his hands to his head.

'You're hurt.' Anji moved towards the stranger.

'No, I'm fine, just a bit dizzy. It was a bit of a bumpy landing, that's all', the boy reassured her.

'"Bit of a bumpy landing?" Is that what you call it? You've pretty much destroyed the pond!'

'Jake, you're not being very helpful,' Anji said as she rummaged around in her bag. 'Hang on; I think I might have something that can help you'.

'Hold on a minute. An alien spaceship falls out of the sky and you're looking for paracetamol! I think I need to sit down, I can't take this all in!' Jake exclaimed.

'Forget about yourself for a moment and help me sit him down.' Anji took the arm of the boy and propped him up.

'But he could be contaminated,' said Jake. 'He could have space mumps or intergalactic flu or something like that.'

'Will you stop being a flump and help!' shouted Anji. Jake straightened himself up instantly and took the other arm of the strange creature. Together, they helped him out of the doorway and onto a nearby rock.

'What's your name?' asked Anji.

'R…andom. My name is Random.'

'Well, you're an alien so how random can it be?' said Jake.

'No. You don't understand,' said the stranger. 'That is my name. My name is Random.'

'Your parents must have loved you then!' Jake felt a sharp punch in his already bruised forearm and saw a stabbing look from Anji.

'Where are you from?' she asked.

'It's too complicated to say right now. You wouldn't understand. I need to rest.'

'No, don't let him go to sleep. When I hit my head on the jungle gym at school Mr Harvison said I might have concussion. Apparently sleep is the worst thing for that.' Jake was finally being of some help.

'No, you can't sleep, Random. We want to help you. Is there anyone else with you?'

'Yes.'

A metallic voice echoed from the smoking chamber and made Anji and Jake jump in surprise.

From the white smoke, a small robot, about two metres in length and around a foot in height, stood in the doorway.

'Bloody hell! A robot, a real robot!' Jake shouted, amazed and delighted all at the same time.

'Actually I am a second generation artificial intelligence service android with a quasi-fissured matrix. Drone class.'

'What does that all mean?' asked Anji.

'Basically speaking Madam, it means I'm a robot.' The AI rolled out of the doorway and with a soft, wet plop embedded himself in the marshy ground. 'Now let me have a look at him.'

A neon blue light skimmed out of the front part of the robot's frame and flickered over Random's nearly unconscious body.

'He is in a state of shock but otherwise there are no minor or immediate danger points on his internal or external physiognomy.' The robots voice was polite, friendly but most of all to the point. 'I think we should let him rest for a while and then hopefully he will be back to his old self. Please could you carry him inside the Venus II?'

'What, you want us to take him inside the spaceship?' Anji was unsure. 'How do we know that you won't abduct us or that there's an army of spacemen in there ready to attack us?'

'Oh, sure, now you ask those kinds of questions,' thought Jake.

'I can assure you that neither Sir nor I mean you any harm. Now please, if you could escort Sir to the ship, I'll deal with the smoke.'

The little robot whizzed off, his wheels picking up the sludge on the ground as he ventured back towards the crash site.

'Cool! We get to go inside a spaceship. This is amazing!' Jake nearly tore off Random's arm as he raced towards the door, momentarily forgetting that he was still clasping hold of the alien boy. Random groaned in protest.

'Wait a second. I'm all for new experiences and adventures but I hardly expected a crashed spaceship with a purple boy and a talking plank of metal today.' Anji stayed motionless on the rock, her trepidation overriding her excitement.

'Come on, Anji. They seem fine. I'm pretty sure that if that robot meant to zap us to death he wouldn't be using words like "please" now would he?'

'You've got a point,' Anji smiled. 'Alright then, let's see what's inside.'

A whirr of internal engines roared from within the fallen craft. The smoke that had once poured from the mouth of the ship disappeared.

'The air conditioning has been initiated. The poisonous gas has now been taken care of. It is safe for you to enter the chamber.'

'Poisonous? Well, that's a relief,' Anji uttered sarcastically.

The duo approached with caution as they entered the Venus II. With Random dragging his feet between them, they found it a struggle to get the alien boy back inside the ship but when they did, they nearly dropped him to the floor in shock and wonderment. It was like nothing they had ever seen before.

The mid-section was an utter mess. An assortment of crockery, chairs and random appliances lay strewn at their feet. Anji looked up and saw what had been the floor before the accident. The table top grazed her head as she walked past it.

'Sorry about the mess but I haven't had a chance to clear up,' said Skateboard apologetically. 'Now, please could you put the Captain somewhere comfortable for the time being? Make yourselves at home - I've got some diagnostics I have to run.'

'What's your name?' asked Anji as she and Jake lay Random down. Jake found a nearby pillow and rested the alien's head against it.

'My real name is GH649Y9D0W but my given name is Skateboard.'

'Can we just call you by your given name?'

said Jake.

'If you so wish,' said Skateboard as he whirred up towards the cockpit.

'How come you weren't injured?' Anji said as she followed the robot. Jake stayed where he was to look over Random, who had now fallen into a deep sleep.

'My exoskeleton is compatible with the electromagnetic hull of this ship,' said Skateboard. 'Unfortunately, Sir was not as lucky. All he could do was stay buckled in and hope for the best.'

'What are you doing here?' Anji walked into the seat buckles that dangled like cobwebs from the cockpit above.

'Well, I guess you could say that we are refugees.'

'Why? What happened?'

'We come from a planet a long way from here. It has suffered centuries of war. Our unconscious friend was wanted by a man called Kalor Maloso so we escaped.'

'Why was he wanted? What had he done?'

'Would it be possible if we could leave the questions for later, Madam? I may be a "robot" but I still need to concentrate.'

'Sorry, it's just all so much to take in,' exclaimed Anji. She left Skateboard to it and walked back into the mid-section. Jake was sitting, mouth wide open, taking in his surroundings.

'This is incredible. Unbelievably cool! Anj, what's the cockpit like?'

'Apart from upside down? All shades of amazing.' Anji sat down next to the prone figure of their new, purple friend. 'What are they doing here? And how on earth are we going to explain all of this to Miss?'

'Miss?' Skateboard interrupted, pulling himself through to the mid-section.

'I thought you had diagnostics to run?' Anji said.

'I did. But they are done now.'

'How come you were so fast?' asked Jake.

Skateboard's hydraulics sighed. 'I am a robot,' he replied. 'Now, please, what do you mean by Miss?'

'Miss Carter. She's our Geography teacher,' said Anji.

'Oh my…' Skateboard shot through to the cockpit again. His circuitry a fluster, he proceeded to connect to the ship's main computer and implored its damaged circuits to turn on the cloaking device.

'This is not good…this is not good at all.' Skateboard muttered to himself. He whizzed past the doorway, the velocity of his hastiness knocking Jake to the floor as he disappeared down the corridor into the main engine bay. Within seconds he was back again.

'The cloaking device is damaged. It's going to take a while to repair. Please, I beg you, go back to your teacher and tell her not to come near here.'

'Children?'

Jake and Anji's faces went white.

'Oh my god. She's coming!' Anji made for the door, her heart pounding like a bass drum in her chest.

'Erm...Anji.'

'What?!'

'Random's not there anymore,' said Jake.

Anji turned towards the door that they had entered the ship through. It was open. She ran towards it, poked her head through the door leading out into the reality of the decimated forest and saw Random in the distance, wobbling his way towards the unseen voice of the teacher.

III

The sound of a crashing aircraft had startled Miss Carter so vigorously that she had dropped her cigarette in the mud. When the ground shook as the craft had smashed into the soft, muddy ground, she had fallen to the floor, her face narrowly missing a nearby puddle but plunging nose first into a stale pile of cow dung. She rose to her feet, spat the nastiness out of her mouth, gagged uncontrollably for a few minutes and then, whilst wiping the excrement off her features, ran hysterically into the woods.

She had let the children go, without supervision, into a wood that had just become a disaster scene. The emergency services would never have failed to pick the crash up on their monitors. All kinds of people would soon be here, she imagined.

Firefighters, ambulances, police…hell, even the army for all she knew! If any of her students would have been caught up in this, she'd never be able to forgive herself.

And it would spell the end of her career as a teacher.

'Children!'

She hollered, her lungs straining against the breath that was quickly escaping her, her legs carrying her further and further into the woods. Further towards her students...and potentially, further towards danger.

'Miss? Miss, what on earth was that?' Jemima Wright had taken shelter in a bush, along with several of the other school children.

'Jemima?' Miss Carter wheezed. 'Oh, thank god, you're all alright.'

'Why are you covered in sh...?'

'...it's nothing!' the children giggled. Miss Carter felt naked. Her class started giggling at her, and not for the first time. On the last school trip, she had lost her footing and fallen into a lake. When she was substituting for a colleague who taught Science and who had taken a sudden leave of absence, she had accidentally set fire to her own trousers with a Bunsen burner, much to the utter delight of the hoard of laughing children. She cursed her clumsiness.

'How many of you are there? Come out of the bush now, we're safe, I'm certain.'

'Safe? I smell bull,' said Ben Wright. The students collapsed in laughter again.

'For goodness sake, so what if I slipped and fell in some poo,' Miss Carter screamed.

'There's been an accident. People could be seriously hurt...or worse. So for the last time, come out and stay close to me.'

The children stopped their juvenile hysterics and fell out of the bush into the pathway. Miss Carter counted with her index finger, catching her breath and found her composure.

'Right, so we are missing three students. James, Anji and Jake. Has anyone seen them?'

'No, Miss,' Jemima replied.

'Right, I want you all to go back to the coach. Inform the driver what has happened and get him to call 999. I only hope that they are okay.'

'Why don't we just call them now? I mean, what if the people in the plane are hurt…or dead!' Ben was being his usual, less than helpful self.

'Not now, Ben,' said Miss Carter. The last thing she needed was the prospect of a worst case scenario.

'It was a big crash, Miss. Look.'

Ben showed his teacher the footage he had captured on his mobile phone. She cleaned her poo-smeared glasses and witnessed what her least favourite pupil had caught on camera.

The footage showed the children larking about, playing with large sticks and pretending that

they were lightsabers.

She could hear a roar on the audio and suddenly, Ben's filming had been directed skywards and Miss Carter was shocked to see a sleek, silver craft shoot through the cracks in the trees. It didn't look like any airplane she had ever seen before. The clip finished with the children screaming in panic.

'Blimey! It's a good thing I gave you your phones back. Okay, give me ten minutes. If I haven't come back to the coach by then, call the emergency services. I'll see you all back at the car park. If you find the park rangers then let them know.'

'How are we supposed to tell when ten minutes is up?' enquired Jemima.

'Use your phones!' shouted Miss Carter.

'Oh yeah,' said Ben.

The teacher tore off into the woods, hollering for the trio of missing students as the children walked back the other way.

'Why does she want us to wait for ten minutes?' asked Jemima.

'Why do you think? She doesn't want to get sacked, does she? If Jake, Anji and 'speccy' kid are brown bread then she'll be fired quicker than a Ferrari in a tunnel.'

Jemima bit her lip hard. 'Do you think they will be alright?'

'Who cares?' said Ben. 'I'm wonder how many hits I can get when I upload this video.'

*

'Random, come back!'

Anji and Jake tore off towards the groggy alien.

'I'm fine, I'm fine, just a bit woozy, that's all,' insisted Random. 'I'll feel fine in a couple of minutes. Fresh air, that's what I need.'

As he walked a little further he could make out the hazy figure of somebody running towards him. He squinted, shook his head and rubbed his eyes to get a better focus. It looked like an adult figure and it was getting closer and closer. They were cursing as their hair and bag kept getting caught up in the brambles and branches that lay in their path, slowing them down but not slow enough for them to miss the sight of Random staggering towards them.

'Oh…' he uttered. Before he had a chance to do anything, his speech was muzzled by the sudden trap of fabric that fell down over his head.

The duo had caught up with him just before Miss Carter managed to see who the strange purple skinned boy was.

'Don't say a word; just let us do the talking,' hissed Anji into Random's ear.

'Say what?' he asked, almost choking on the hood chord that had climbed into his throat.

'There you are! I've been worried sick!' Miss Carter's lungs were practically on fire. Her secret smoking habit, coupled with a lack of physical exercise, made her light headed and tired. She rested down on her haunches. She coughed a deep, sludgy cough, the tar shifting in the back of her throat.

'Blimey, you'll be sick in a moment if you don't breathe,' said Jake sarcastically.

'We're fine, Miss,' reassured Anji. 'Absolutely fine. How is everyone else?'

When she had regained her breath, Miss Carter managed to summon up enough energy to speak.

'Everyone else is safe and accounted for. Did you see what happened? And why has James stuffed his coat over his face?'

Anji's heart started pumping a little faster.

'He…er…'

'…he's a little upset…about the crash.'

Oh no, thought Anji. She had just realised that they would have to fabricate two lies on the spot: 1) the identity of the alien, which had already been taken care off for the immediate future and 2) the crashed spaceship behind them.

Miss Carter jumped to her feet, ignoring the stitch that felt like a dagger on fire had imbedded itself in her left ribcage and pleaded wild eyed to her pupils.

'Oh, I almost forgot when I saw you, where is it? Are there any survivors? How am I going to explain this to the Headmaster?'

'Where is what?' Anji looked quizzically at her frantic teacher. Surely something like a giant silver spaceship, big enough to destroy a pond which will probably lay deep in the woods for centuries, couldn't go unnoticed. Especially as the crash site was a mere fifty metres or so behind them.

She turned tentatively to look over her shoulder and at the same time both Jake and Random - or 'James' - did exactly the same thing.

It was gone. The Venus II had gone. It was nowhere to be seen and bizarrely the pond was still there. Sure, it looked a little bigger and there appeared to be a path of broken trees, fallen pine cones and other foliage, but the offending article had been removed. Or had it?

Skateboard! That brilliant little machine had done it. The Venus II was still there, but it had cloaked itself. To Miss Carter, or anyone else who ventured near, there was nothing to see that hadn't been there before.

'Er...no idea, Miss.'

'Right, well since I've found you three I think the next best thing would be to let the local authorities deal with it. Let's only hope it wasn't as bad as the video depicts.'

'What video?' asked Jake.

'Ben caught the 'crash' – or whatever it was – on camera,' said Miss Carter. 'Now don't worry about that. We can only be thankful that we are all alive and well.'

And that some of us have kept our jobs, thought the teacher.

Random was still feeling worse for wear but he had recovered enough to play along at this point. In the immediate instance, it was best to keep quiet and keep himself hidden as much as he could from view. Thank goodness the coat that he had forced upon him was full length, protecting his arms and legs and his less than orthodox clothes out of sight. Suddenly, he picked up on a pungent stench coming from the woman standing in front of him. It smelt terrible and he couldn't help sniffing loudly.

'Oh, don't worry, James, it will all okay. Miss has got you,' she cooed.

Random struggled to understand what she was on about but shook his head anyway, playing along with the others.

'We'll look after him,' Jake said, forcing his arm around Random's shoulders and shaking him vigorously.

'Hmm...that's good of you Jake. Especially

after what you two have gone through lately. It's nice for the pair of you to put your differences to one side in times of need. Come on then, back to the coach. I'm sure the police will want to talk to us.'

'Oh...okay.' Anji was starting to feel like a bag of nerves. As they walked away from the pond, a number of questions started circulating in her mind. Were they really about to smuggle an alien back to their school? Where were they going to hide him? Mores to the point, how on earth were they going to get him back to his ship? And what if that Maloso guy followed Random to earth and was still looking for him? She looked behind her, where the Venus II had once been. She prayed that Skateboard was looking out at them and had a better plan than either she or Jake had.

'It's turned out to be a weird day, hasn't it? said Miss Carter.

'Oh,' whispered Anji under her breath. 'You have no idea.'

*

Skateboard watched the scenes unfold on the monitor.

Despite the crash, the ship had held up well.

Well, that's to be expected when the craft is made up of seda metal - the toughest metal compound in the known universe - and titanium - the runner-up in the toughest metal compound in all the known universe competition.

He looked on, helpless, as his Captain was led away with this unknown species. Skateboard knew deep down in his motherboard that Random would be alright, but what to do now? Await his return? He couldn't do that. A beeping signal from the sonic scope alarmed the AI. Pouring over its findings, he discovered that a swarm was heading his way. Imploring the computer for more information, the swarm appeared to be an oncoming juggernaut of vehicles. Skateboard panicked. This meant more trouble. He plugged himself into the main computer and searched the binary for a full diagnostic of damage to the Venus II. Luckily, despite the ship being upside down, 89% of the hull and its internal circuits were intact. Luck seemed to be on Skateboard's side.

He disconnected himself from the computer and hooked himself up to the tracking system. The Venus II was a very special ship indeed. As soon as a living organism sets foot on board, the ship makes a biological imprint, meaning that they can be tracked wherever they go within a 500-mile radius.

Skateboard made sure that the imprints of

Random and the two children who had helped him were recorded. So now, he knew where they were, so when the time was right, he could rescue his friend. But first, he had to move the Venus II.

He peered over the sonic scope again. The swarm was getting closer.

Roughly five miles away now.

He could also pick up heat signatures and he could tell that although there seemed to be several bodies leaving the woods, more were on their way.

There was no time to lose.

'Computer - pilot code GH649Y9D0W - full control.'

The ship whirred into life with a cough and a splutter. Skateboard could now control the whole ship, just through the power of his will.

He fired the retros up. The ship began to wriggle; the nose section began receding from the hole in the pond. Slowly but surely, the Venus II began to pull itself away from the crash site. Skateboard initiated his electromagnetic capabilities and instructed the ship to flip over to its correct position. The ship rattled like a salt shaker as it completed the maneuver. Skateboard instructed the rockets underneath the ship to fire upwards, propelling the ship through the trees it hadn't destroyed before piloting the craft away from the crash site.

Meanwhile, whilst Anji and Jake helped "James" on board the coach; they overheard the din of engines in the near distance. Random, with the coat still disguising his appearance, knew it was Skateboard fleeing the site.

His head bowed, disconsolate, hoping that his friend would be able to find him soon as he stepped onto the coach and was ushered to a window seat by Anji, who took up the seat next to him. A blizzard of noise blazed away. An entourage of cars, fire engines and ambulances sped into the car park. Miss Carter stepped off the coach. Jake saw her approach one of the police officers, straining to make out what she was saying to him through the glass window. He shot a panicked look to Anji, who held onto Random's arm.

'Don't worry; we'll get you out of this. I promise.'

'Right kids,' said the coach driver. 'I've just been told that Miss Carter will be assisting the police in their enquiries.'

His speech was halted when a policeman stepped up onto the coach.

'Right, please listen up children; I just wanted to reassure you that everything is in hand and your coach driver will be taking you back to your school in due course. We just need to ask your teacher some questions first. She'll be meeting you further on down the road – we need to evacuate this area in case of any danger to civilians. Thank you for your understanding.'

Just as he went to step off again, Ben's phone started to vibrate.

'Hello Mum! No, I'm fine, why's that? What! No way!'

'What's up?' asked Anji.

'My video's been shown on the news! I only uploaded it a few minutes ago!'

'What are they saying?'

Ben repeated the question into the mobile. 'They are saying it's a possible plane crash.'

The children gasped in horror.

'I'm pretty sure it isn't,' said Jake.

'Yeah, it could be aliens!' said Jemima.

The children began screaming.

The policeman strode down the gangway, walking past Random and snatched the phone off Ben.

'Hello, who is this? Mrs Wright, I'd just like to reassure you that your son and his classmates are safe. We will be moving them on soon…what's that?

No, no aliens…well, no I haven't seen the crash site yet…I think that we can safely say that there are no aliens in the vicinity.'

He handed the phone back to Ben.

'And let me repeat that to all of you. We don't want to scaremonger. For all we know it might just be a crashed drone. One thing we can definitely rule out is that it is aliens that we are dealing with. Thank you.'

And with that, the policeman stepped off the coach.

Anji started shaking in fear. What had they got themselves into? She shared a knowing look with Jake, who looked equally as nervous and looked over to Random. Through the hood, she could see his red/blue eyes looking back at her, helpless and scared.

About ten minutes later, Miss Carter, her witness statement safely with the police, rejoined her class and the coach pulled away back to London. Little did they know that there was an illegal alien on board, and the boy whose identity he had adopted, was still lost in the woods.

IV

How Anji and Jake ever smuggled Random back to their home, they will never know. The whole afternoon was a blur. As soon as the coach pulled up at the school, they managed to hide Random, still swathed in Jake's parker jacket, past the line and into the cloak room, where Miss Carter had interrogated the pair on what they had seen in the woods.

Before long, the local police had also gone round to class 3B. Each student was called up to give an account as to what they had seen, but the duo decided that they would quietly slip away at the earliest possible opportunity and escape to the relative safety of their home.

They did just that, picking Random up out of the cloakroom, before catching the school bus back to their sanctuary.

Anji almost snapped the key in the lock since she was in such a rush to enter. Random had glimpsed through the hood at the house. It was a rather new house; the bricks were an oblique grey. The house stood three stories high. Random had never seen anything like it. It was like a palace to him.

Eventually, they made it to Anji's room. After

climbing up the 2 flights of stairs, they reached the top floor and burst through the bedroom door, almost tearing it from its hinges in the process. The trio collapsed on the single bed, breathless and relieved.

'Oh my god, how on earth did we just do that?' Jake enquired.

'What do you mean?' said Anji.

'Well, we just smuggled an alien from Dartmoor to school and then half way across London!'

'Maybe someone up there is looking over us?' Anji suggested.

'Ugh.'

Random groaned. He began to tear at the parker's restrictive fabric.

'Hold on a minute, let me pull the blinds first! Just in case anyone is looking in at us.'

'Like who?' asked Jake, thinking that Anji was being overly paranoid given they were on the second floor. 'No, don't tell me: Simon Formby?'

Simon was an unpopular child in Anji's Math's class. His chunky spectacles, unsightly acne and terrible body odour made him the least desirable boy in Year 3.

Classmates had been known to avoid him at all costs for prolonged periods like lessons time, especially after learning that one of the giant zits on his cheek had erupted like a volcano of teenage sebum and dirt into the face of poor Samantha Ripley. From that moment on, Simon was scorned and Samantha never ate mayonnaise again.

Unfortunately for Anji, he harboured strong feelings for her. Despite the love letters, the little gifts left pinned to her school locker and the god-awful poetry, Anji's affections were not forthcoming. Awkwardly for her, he lived right across the road and was prone to looking out for her after school.

Anji peered out of the window down to the road below and sure enough, there was Simon, looking up at the top window which belonged to her bedroom. When he saw Anji looking, he waved his fingers in a 'come hither' way. She grunted and snapped the blinds shut.

'Forget about him, we've got more important things to think about,' she said as they helped Random out of his disguise.

Now things had calmed down, they could see him for who he truly was.

'My god, you're so purple,' said Jake. 'Why is that? Is it a birthmark?'

'I guess so,' said Random.

'How are you feeling now?'

'Fine thanks. I don't think I caught your names?'

'Well, I'm Jake. And as an ambassador for the planet Earth…'

Anji jabbed Jake sharply in the ribs.

'My name is Anji', she replied to Random.

'Anji. You saved me, didn't you?'

'Well, we both did, thank you very much!' corrected Jake.

'I'm thankful. I really am. You wouldn't believe the day I'd had.' Random's mind still felt cloudy. He remembered the escape from Rodas, Maloso and the Sandman. He just could not remember the events of his 'landing' on this planet 'Earth'.

'What happened?'

Anji filled him in on the details. 'We were on a school trip. A really boring one until you turned up! Then we heard a crash so we ran to the place where it came from and saw you staggering outside of a spaceship.'

Shaking the last of his groggy state from his head, Random suddenly now remembered everything that had happened since his escape from Rodas. The crash, the two stangers, Skateboard and the Venus II leaving him behind…

'Oh no! The Venus II and Skateboard; they've left me here!!'

A sea of panic washed over Random's features.

'Don't worry!'

'They've left me alone!'

'We'll look after you now, please, keep your voice down,' Anji implored.

'Keep my voice down? I've just been abandoned on an alien world and you're asking me to keep my voice down?' Random shot up from the bed, making the teenagers jump.

'Hey, you're the alien here, buddy, not us,' said Jake.

'We'll help you find your way back to the crash site, I promise,' Anji's tone soothed Random.

'Well, what do we do in the meantime?'

'You can stay here.'

'Woah, I don't think Jason will agree,' said Jake.

'Who is Jason?'

'He takes care of us. This is a care home.'

Random started to calm his nerves a little.

'Why should you help me? You don't know me. And why should you trust me. I am an 'alien' after all,' Random shot a look to Jake.

'Look, I'm sorry about that. I'm sure we can work something out, even if we have to keep you a secret up here. Don't worry, we can bring you food.'

'Sounds like you want to keep me in captivity,' said Random.

'Of course not,' assured Anji. 'It'll only be until we can find Skateboard again.'

Random sat back down on the bed, feeling the soft duvet under the palms of his hands.

'We won't tell anybody you're here. It'll be fun.'

'It doesn't sound very fun,' scoffed Random.

'Please. We really want to help you; friends?'

As a sign of friendship, Anji held out her hand. She willed Random to shake it. He did. He pinched her thumb and pulled it up and down in a rocking motion.

'Friends,' smiled Random.

Jake didn't know whether to laugh or not.

'Right; so how big is the planet 'Earth.' Where is it?'

'I can help you out with this one. Lie back,' said Anji as she joined Random on the bed. Random did as he was asked and let the back of his head sink into the firm mattress.

'You see those planets up there?'
Anji pointed to her ceiling. Along with the congealed blobs of blu tack staining the white finish, there were pictures of worlds that Random had never seen before.

'I meant to take these down ages ago. The person I inherited this room from was a big fan of spacey stuff.'
She motioned her finger towards the blue/green

planet.
That one there...that's us, three along from the sun. That's the planet Earth. If you squint, you can make out a tiny island near the top of the world.

Random fixed his eyes upon it.

'That's where we are. That's the United Kingdom.'

Jake sat in the chair, gawking up at the ceiling, like his friends.

'Wow,' Random seemed genuinely interested. 'How many people live in the United Kingdom?'

'We covered this the other day,' said Jake. 'There are just over 65 million people.'

'How many?! On one tiny island? How do you all fit?'

'Some would argue we don't,' said Anji. She sighed, remembering some of the jibes she had endured in the past from ignorant classmates.

'It's amazing. Do you all live in places like this?'

'The lucky ones do,' said Jake. 'The majority of people live with their families.'

'What are families?'

'Y'know, Mums and Dads with their children. Do you have a Mum and Dad?'

'No. At least I don't think so.'

Anji looked quizzical. 'Are you an orphan?'

'What's that?'

'It's what we are. We don't have a Mum or Dad,' Jake explained.

'No, I'm not an orphan,' Random replied.

'So how old are you?' asked Anji.

'I'm not very old. In fact, I'm roughly 2 moon circles old.'

'You're two days old? Christ, you've aged!' said Jake.

'I don't think my biological make-up is anything like yours. I'm an 'alien' remember?' Random shot another look at Jake. He was beginning to wonder if they would end up getting on at all.

'Tell us all about it,' asked Anji.

As they lied on the bed, Random told Anji and Jake everything.

He opened up about his early beginnings; how his first memory is stepping out of a glass tube, fully formed and seeing the destruction and bloodshed that surrounded him.

He retold the story of his escape. How the Crimson Empire had hunted him down like an animal and the unlikely desertion, when he used his strength to throw the heli-fighter away like a paper plane.

'Wow, remind me never to challenge you to an arm wrestle,' said Jake.

He opened his heart to the recollection of seeing the refugees of war, staring at him, helplessness burning in their souls. Anji could see a tear in his eye, making her also well up with emotion. Even Jake bowed his head solemnly.

Random continued, telling his new companions about how the Sandman had taken him in as an unwanted house guest, the discovery of the Venus II, Skateboard, the escape from Rodas and the feeling of abandoning those people.

'Oh, Random,' cooed Anji, blinking away the tears. 'No wonder you ran off.'

'I don't blame you either. There's nothing you could have done,' said Jake, who was also welling up.

'That's what Skateboard said, oh, I miss that little guy.'

'I'll go get us some food from the kitchen. I don't think any of the other kids are back yet. We're the youngest here so many of them will be at the youth club on a Friday night. So we should have the pick of the grub!'

Jake swiveled on the office chair and made for the door.

Anji held Random's hand and smiled at him.

'You've got us now. We'll help you however we can.'

Random smiled. 'I wonder what he is getting up to now.'

*

High above the cities financial superpowers and the tower blocks that glistened in the evening sun, Skateboard had parked the Venus II on top of the tallest building in London. Here, he had spent the last 130 kels, or two hours in human time as he understood it, to carry out the necessary repairs on the ship. Before choosing on his hideout, he carried out a scan on the area. Random was less than 15 miles away.

Skateboard had chosen the spot so that he could keep a close eye on his Captain; not so that he could look out at the local scenery. Beautiful though it was, with the River Thames shimmering in the glow of the oncoming night and Big Ben, which seemed to incessantly chime every 60th kels, or hour in human time as he understood it, the little AI, ironically, just didn't have the time to take any of it in. He hadn't even had the time to inspect the mysterious white circular attraction on the river bank.

Instead, the 'robot' as the blonde human had called him, was busy at work until something abruptly broke his focus.

'Hello? Is anyone here?'

Skateboard froze.

'Hello?'

There it was again, that same, shrill voice.

He checked the internal scanner. It had been on the blink since the crash in the woods but now, it was starting to work again. There in the centre of the picture, was a figure getting closer and closer.

Skateboard's optical circuits whirled.

There, in the doorway stood another school boy. One whom Skateboard didn't recognise.

The AI didn't know whether to continue his silence or to speak. Stupidly, he went for the latter.

'Can I be of any assistance, Master?'

The boy jumped.

'Gosh. A robot! Wow!'

'Actually I am a…no, forget it I don't have the time to go through that now. Who are you and why are you on my ship?'

'My name's James. James Butcher. I'm with the school trip.' James tore around the cockpit like a cricket in a summer meadow.

'Wow! I can't believe it. This is so cool. I had no idea they were filming in these woods!'

'What are you talking about, young Sir?'

'Well, this is a film set, isn't it? Look at the special effects.' He motioned for the switches on the control unit behind the co-pilot's chair.

'Don't touch that, Sir.'

'Why not?'

'Because if you did, your oxygen supply would be instantly cut off.'

James laughed.

'Yeah…of course. So who is controlling you then?'

'No-one is controlling me, Sir.'

'There must be some guy who is acting out your voice. Are you famous in real life?'

Why was this child asking such stupid questions?

'I have no idea what you are talking about.'

'Also, where are Jake and Anji? I followed them here but I have been all over the set and I still can't see them. Never mind, it all looks so convincing! Especially when you "took-off",' James made quotation signs with his fingers, 'this is utterly immense!'

Skateboard decided to save face and go along with it.

'Sir, I'm sorry to disappoint you but Jake and Anji have gone home. I think you should go home too.'

'What? No way am I going home yet. I want to meet the stars.'

James bounded off into the mid-section. Skateboard wondered if there was any chloroform in the munitions cabinet. If he could knock the boy unconscious, making sure he didn't harm him, and then broke cover to drop him off back in the woods, he would. Then he could get on with his work in peace and the boy would believe that all of this was just a dream.

He hoped.

'Sir, would you mind just coming into the cockpit for a moment? I need to go and…er…find the masters from the film.'

'Wow, really…wow. Sorry, I say wow a lot when I'm excited.'

'I hadn't noticed,' said Skateboard. *Please, mercy, let there be chloroform on board!*

James moved forward from the mid-section and felt a crunch under his foot.

'Whoops. Sorry.'

'What is that?' asked Skateboard.

'Oh, just a puddle of sand I stepped in. There are a few puddles of it down that corridor.' James pointed. The puddles of sand he was referring too were not there anymore.

To his shock and horror, the 'puddle' began to shake. A solid form began erecting towards the ceiling.

James opened his mouth to scream but he couldn't make a sound, his larynx paralysed by fear.

Skateboard quaked in his mechanical boots.

'No. This is impossible.'

The grains continued to collate together. The image of a man began to form.

Skateboard was stunned. There must have been some granules still on board when he and Random left Rodas.

Fully regenerated, standing before the pair was a man made of sand.

V

Skateboard and James cowered at the giant intruder who had seemingly just materialised aboard the Venus II. With eyes of silt, the Sandman blinked back into existence. His brow bore a frowned expression, one of sheer determination and frustration. Before long, he spoke.

'Miss me?'

Skateboard began to whirr, his circuitry disabling all the protocols that gave the Sandman voice activation control of the ship.

'Well…did you?' the Sandman spat grains from the corners of his mouth.

James stared up at the stranger in shock.

'Wow…did you just see that? What is the budget for this thing?'

'I regret to inform you that I did not.' Skateboard's etiquette was still annoyingly impeccable.

'I didn't think you did. Still, I suppose I should hand it to you really, my little pet. You did get me off Rodas after all.'

'Not exactly; Your metaphysical imprint is stretched between here and there. You have regenerated through the aspects of your DNA that were left on board.

The medical scanners on the ship must have resurrected your imprint here by accident. So, basically speaking, you're not even half the man you once were.'

'Good exposition. Who scripted this thing?' asked James.

The Sandman's patience was being tested to breaking point.

'Shut up! Sit over there and don't say another word until I say so.'

James did exactly as he was told and took up residence on the sofa. All of a sudden, he felt a shard of fear trickle down his spine. Either this was great method acting, or something even stranger was going on here. For the time being, and for the integrity of his own insanity, he plumped for the former.

The Sandman slowly made for Skateboard. The little AI noticed that his former "master" was limping slightly. His physical state was severely impaired. He also noticed that his form was not as solid as before. You might even say that the Sandman looked almost transparent as he moved under the warm glow of the interior lighting rig.

As he tipped his head downwards towards the robot, several grains of sand fell like coarse snow onto Skateboard's bodywork.

'Where is he?' the Sandman bellowed.

*

Random lay awake on the floor of Anji's room listening to the soft snore emanating from the bed above him. This whole planet felt weird. It was night time and yet it was much, much darker than the daytime, something that Random had grown used to during his short stay on his home planet.

After dinner, which consisted of something called "chicken and chips" (a delicacy which Random actually rather liked), Jake decided to introduce Random to something called a "first person shooter." He had enjoyed his turn on the "Xbox" but Anji scorned her blonde friend saying that he was being, "insensitive, especially after everything Random has told us!"

And so they had moved on to a game that involved a sport called football. Random enjoyed this experience much more, although he found the concept of eleven men facing a further eleven men trying to kick a ball into a net, with almost the entire side forbidden to touch the ball with their hands.

An alien concept, indeed.

He sighed as he continued to stare up at the ceiling from his makeshift bed covers.

Anji had offered him her bed but he didn't fancy sleeping there. It was hers, after all!
Random could not take his eyes off the twinkling stars that blinked above him. He dreamed of the planets which all looked down upon him; Mercury, Venus, Earth, Mars, Jupiter, Uranus, Saturn and Neptune.

Rolling over and closing his eyes, he began thinking about Skateboard and how he longed to see the AI and the Venus II again, until he drifted off into a blissful, deep sleep.

'Anj…'

Jake knocked again on the door.

'Anj! Come on!'

The door creaked open. Anji, wearing a pink night dress and her hair mated over her tired eyes, poked her head through the crack.

'Wow, aren't you a sight for sore eyes.'

'Shut up and get in,' Anji instructed.

Jake did as he was told. Carrying a tray of toast, jam and tea, he entered the bedroom, stepped over Random's sleeping body and rested the tray tentatively on the desk.

'Did you sleep well?' he asked.

'Like a baby,' said Anji. She rubbed the sleep from her eyes and let out a big yawn.

'Yourself?'

'Surprisingly, yes I did. Although I did have a

terrible dream in the night; I dreamt that we'd been on a school trip, picked up an alien refugee and you were hiding him under your bed.'

'Well, I hate to break it to you, mate, but either you're still dreaming or you've woken up in a nightmare,' she smiled.

'Ah come on, it's not so bad.'

'Not so bad? What'll happen when the school finds out that James didn't come back with us? We'll be the first people they come to looking for him. Who is to say that hasn't happened already? For all we know his parents could be on the phone to our school right now.' Anji began to look worried.

'Of course they won't be. It's Saturday, remember? No one goes to school on a Saturday!' Jake pointed at Random. 'Do you think he will want some breakfast?'

'I'm not sure. Do aliens eat breakfast?'

'Who knows,' scoffed Jake as he devoured a slice of toast. 'But I'm having his.'

'Why didn't you make your own?'

'I did.'

'Then why are you eating his?'

'Hey, I'm still hungry.'

'Go and get some more, for goodness sake!'

Jake put the half eaten toast back on the plate and retreated back to the door with the tray.

As Anji shut the door behind him, Random sprang into life. His eyes opened with the haste of a lightning bolt and he jumped out of the covers like a jack in the box, uncoiled and yawned like a lion calling for his pack.

'Right, what did I miss?'

'Breakfast apparently,' said Anji. She opened her laptop and decided to brave it and see what social media had to say about the crash.

The story was everywhere.

MYSTERY OF CRASHED "PLANE" the news outlets screamed. Ben's video had not only gone viral. It had gone global. As she continued to read the stories, it became apparent that some of their classmates had exaggerated the situation and made up tales about how the ship nearly killed them. There were also terrible lies being spread.

'AN ARMY OF ALIENS ATTACKED US, I SAW IT!' claimed Sadie Long.

'HE SAID, "WE COME IN PEACE" AND THEN EVAPORATED INTO THIN AIR,' asserted Ross Wilkinson.

'HE WANTED TO PHONE HOME…BUT WE ENDED UP SWAPPING NUMBERS,' declared Jemima Wright.

'Oh, I hate that girl so much!' Anji spat.

'So...we might have caused a bit of a scene then, eh?' enquired Random.

Anji nodded.

'Right, well at least nobody knows we are here'.

Like a storm cloud gathering over the Notting Hill Carnival, something was about to rain on the youngster's parade.

Meanwhile, Jake was busying himself in the kitchen, making another round of toast for his new friend upstairs. Humming to himself, he was blissfully unaware that Jason was standing in the doorway, watching him.

'You're not normally up this early,' he said.

'Oh! Jason, you startled me. Yes, I erm…couldn't sleep last night.' Jake dropped the buttered piece of toast to the floor. In a bizarre moment on improbability, the toast landed butter side up for the first time in the history of mankind.

'It wouldn't have anything to do with this…alien thing, now would it?'

Jake scoffed. 'No, of course not. What alien thing?'

Jason walked closer to Jake, who was busying himself with yet another round of toast, completely ignoring the abandoned slice lying at his feet.

'Come on Jake, you're not fooling me. You were on the trip that has been cited by

NewsCorp as 'Star Trekkers.'

So come on then, spill the beans.'

'I didn't see anything,' Jake lied.

Jason stood a tall six foot one and his broad physique towered imposingly over the teen.

'Are you sure?'

Jake tried his hardest to keep the truth from his carer.

He was failing miserably.

'Yep. Absolutely. I mean, they didn't find anything did they? Plus, any idiot can use an editing suite nowadays to make any old rubbish up.'

Jason blinked down on the child.

'Really?'

Jason moved into the hallway.

'Then would you be so kind as to tell this lot!'

He opened the front door.

There outside, a large number of keen journalists had gathered, desperate to hear the story first hand. A myriad of flashing lights and frenzied questions hit Jake like a ton of bricks.

The boy stood aghast at the commotion.

A sea of hacks awaited him.

'Could you tell us if you're hording aliens?'

'Can you explain to us the mystery of the plane...was it a plane?'

'Have you come into contact with extra-terrestrial life forms after your school trip?'

Jake dropped the tray and ran over to the door, slamming it shut. His eyes, wild with panic darted all around, his mind too slow to assimilate the commotion behind the relative safety of the front door.

'H-how long have they been out there?' he stuttered.

'About an hour or so. Apparently your friends have been posting all kinds about it.'

Jason reached for the telephone.

'I'm calling the police. There's no way we can put up with this.'

'The police? Here?'

Jason scanned Jake's sheet white face.

'Unless there is something you are hiding from me?'

'No! There is absolutely nothing to tell.'

The commotion outside was not the only surprise awaiting the pair.

Out of the blue, Jake's phone started to buzz. He normally left it on silent for two reasons. One, so that he wasn't disturbed by the embarrassing ring tone that Anji once pranked him with and which he now can't seem to change and two, because it never failed to massage his ego when he checked it every now and again and a backlog of missed calls, texts and notifications always made him feel more popular than he really was.

'Sorry, Jason, I've got to take this.'

Jake ran upstairs as fast as his legs could carry him and slammed into his room.

Tentatively, he picked the receiver up.

'Hello?'

'Jake. It's Miss Carter here. It appears we have a problem.'

'Oh?'

'Yes,' Miss Carter sounded unusually calm.

'I've just received a phone call from the school. It's from James' parents. It appears that he didn't return home last night…'

'Ah.'

Jake was perspiring at an alarming rate. He felt like his heart was about to explode. The anxiety levels grew and grew inside his teenage mind. Unsurprisingly, he started to hyperventilate.

'Right…well, you see, the thing is er…Miss…'

Think brain, think. I know we don't seem to be the best of friends most of the time but I really need you now!

'He…was here. Last night. It got late and asked if he could spend the night with us.'

Yes! You've done it, brain. You've done it! I promise not to keep killing you with too much gaming.

'Right,' Miss Carter seemed very unsure. 'So how come he didn't ring his parents?'

You can do it, come on. Just one more time.

'Phone died,' replied Jake.

'And neither of you could lend him a charger?'

Um…

'Jake, I'm waiting.'

Brain, I take it all back. You suck!

'It didn't occur to us at the time, Miss. Anyway, he never even asked us if he could borrow one.'

Jake clenched his teeth. His last excuse was undeniably weak.

'I think I'd better come over and have a word with your carer.'

'Sorry Miss but I'm afraid that-'

Jake's phone died completely. He looked at it. Ironically, it had run out of charge. Instant karma for using that excuse, he thought.

Without a moment's hesitation, he tore away from his room and burst in on Anji's again.

'Guys…we've got trouble…BIG trouble!'

VI

'You're right,' confirmed Random as he peered through the curtains at the melee ensuing below. 'We ARE in big trouble!'

'Right!' Jake was breathing in and out of a paper bag that had once housed Anji's cosmetic stash. 'The school has found out that James is missing, the internet has exploded with rumours and we've got Jason coming up the stairs this minute who is about to find out that we are harbouring an alien!'

'Keep your voice down, Jake, for goodness sake!' Anji hissed.

'Maybe we can reason with him,' said Random.

'What!?'

'Keep blowing Jake,' said Anji. 'What are you suggesting?'

KNOCK KNOCK!

Jake blew so hard that the bag popped like bubble gum.

'Oh crap!'

The teenager shot under Anji's bed.

'Come in,' cooed Random.

Jason stormed through the door. 'Just what on

earth do you kids think you are...'

'It's Jason, isn't it? Come in, come in, and make yourself at home. Although technically you are home, but what the heck, get comfy.'

Anji was taken away by Random's bravado.

'Y-y-you're a...' Jason's eyes opened wider than ever. He was in the presence of a stranger. A purple stranger.

'There you are,' Random ushered him over to the chair.

'Now then, I hear that there is a bit of a commotion going on outside? Well, it's all very simple. You see, I am not an alien. Far from it. I've never even been outside of this country! I'm a wanderer; a nomad of the streets. This skin colour is an unfortunate birthmark and my clothes? Well, if you were homeless too, you'd probably borrow the nearest clothing to hand to cover your nakedness. But let me ask you this? Would you let a homeless boy in an unforgiving world be the subject of a vicious internet rumour? No Mum, no Dad. No friends except those in this room right now? Nobody to defend him?'

Jake peered from his hiding place. This was incredible. Random was talking not just his way out of trouble but his and Anji's too. Was Jason going to buy it?

'How did you get in then?'

'They found me in the woods.'

I don't believe it, thought Anji. *What a clever guy! He wasn't lying. He was manipulating the truth.*

'I had got lost. I'd dawdled for days and found myself in the country. Then I met these two and they saved me and promised to help. I pleaded with them to take me back and to keep me safe.'

Random walked over to the window. There were more vans and press than before, hammering on the door.

'I'm so sorry. I don't want to cause any grief. I just want a roof over my head.'

Jason was taken aback by the story; a boy of the streets. Was he unwanted by his parents and left to fend for himself? Was it because of his deformity? It was unusual to see a boy whose skin was bright purple, but to cast him out was utterly deplorable. Especially to a man who had dedicated his whole adult life to helping the disadvantaged.

'What is your name?' he asked.

'My name is Andrew Smith. At least, that's the name I have given myself.'

Jason sat engrossed in the boy's story.

'Okay, Andrew. Here's what we'll do. I'll go and telephone the police, tell them that there is no cause for alarm and we'll sort out this mess.'

He did just that. Within minutes, the police were on the scene, clearing the crowd with great difficulty at first, but after a while the hacks of Fleet Street eventually scurried back to their offices with no answers to the online rumours that the care home was housing a being from another world.

As the care home was just that, the local constabulary made absolutely certain that the building's location would not be revealed by any journalist.

After the commotion had died down, Detective Inspector Willis, accompanied by two of his officers, Miss Carter and Jason, questioned the children in the kitchen.

Considering their stories were corroborated hastily and that Anji and Jake had taken inspiration from Random's warped tale of events, there was just enough truth in their tale that DI Willis had no choice but to believe them.

They bought it all; Random's story that he has been alone most of his life, that he is a stranger, lost in a boulevard of chaos and that he had met the teenagers in the woods. After what seemed like an age, DI Willis was finally satisfied.

'Alright, there's just one final question I would like to ask. You've told us everything we'd like to know about the boy but there is still the whereabouts of your classmate that we have to worry about.'

DI Willis' stubby fingers reached for a rich tea

biscuit, his seventh since the questioning had commenced. Miss Carter cut him a scornful expression. Rich tea biscuits were her favourite and now they were all gone.

'The fact of the matter is that your actions have led to a missing person. We'll make sure that the local authorities are aware and that the boy's parents are notified of the latest news.'

'Couldn't the staff at the National Park be of any help?' asked Miss Carter.

DI Willis wiped the crumbs from his lips.

'We've already been in contact with the constabulary in the area and he confirmed that there has been no sightings, but don't worry, I'm sure we'll find him.'

'We're so sorry,' said Anji. There was genuine remorse etched over her face.

'I'll leave you to deal with these two.'

DI Willis pulled his bulky frame up from his chair and shook Jason's hand.

'We'll be in touch with any further information as it comes in. We'll see ourselves out. Anything else you youngsters care to share then please let us know as soon as possible. Good day.'

He smiled at the carer and glared at Miss Carter. As the police departed, she could contain her anger no longer.

'What the hell do you think you are playing at?'

'We're really sorry, Miss, sorrier than you can ever know.' Jake looked sheepish as he spoke.

'I am utterly shocked and appalled at the pair of you. How dare you leave a classmate behind? Worse of all lie to me! I knew you were up to something when you ran from school.'

'Miss, if there is anything we can do to help then-'

'Help, Anji? Help! I don't need your help. You have no idea the problems you have caused me. I shall have to answer to the district councilors on Monday. I could lose my job because of this!'

'Miss Carter, I'm sure you will keep your job,' Jason put his hand on her shoulder. The teacher recoiled; acting like his touch was as cold as ice.

'Don't you touch me!' she barked. 'You think your kind words can help the situation. A boy has gone missing!'

'They'll find him, now please, Emily, calm down. The children are truly sorry.'

Emily? Thought Jake. *Who'd have thunk? And how on earth did Jason know her first name?*

'I think you need a good rest. They'll find James, I'm sure of it. It hasn't been twelve hours since you left and that park is big.'

'He could have been eaten by a bear, or kidnapped by an escaped convict!'

'Both are highly unlikely. Now I assure you, Emily, everything will be alright. I promise.'

Jason's eyes smiled at her through his gangly ginger fringe. She smiled back.

'Okay, maybe you're right,' she conceded.

'I know I am. Now, go home and get some rest. I'll show you out.'

Emily Carter got up to leave. She eyed Random with terrible uncertainty. His purple complexion still baffled her.

'I hope you find somewhere that'll take care of you.'

'Thanks for your sentiment,' said Random. There was an element of cheekiness in his voice which made Emily frown.

'As for you two, I want you in my office first thing Monday. I'll have thought what you do with you by then.'

That's it, a year of lunchtime detentions for us, thought Anji.

'Come on,' Jason escorted Emily into the hallway. As they walked to the front door, the trio in the kitchen could hear the couple chatting. They all craned their necks, spying on the adults as they peered around the kitchen door.

Shortly afterwards, they distinctly heard Jason tell their Geography teacher that he'd "be around later," before pecking her on the lips.

As he shut the door, Jason could feel watching eyes burning on the back of his neck. As he turned to face the teenagers, their faces slinked back out of sight.

'What a morning,' he groaned.

'I was telling the truth with what I said, Jason,' said Anji. 'We really are truly sorry.'

'I know you are, kids. I've been here long enough to get to know the pair of you. I know you wouldn't have done this out of intent. I just wish you'd let Emily...I mean, Miss Carter know that you'd found Andrew when you did.'

'I'm not blameless either,' said Random. 'I'm sorry that my presence has brought about this mess.'

Jason looked up at the purple child.

'Look, I can have a word with the local authorities. DI Willis gave me a number to call. I can't promise anything, but I might be able to give you a roof over your head.'

'You mean,' Jake felt a wave of optimism wash over him, 'he can stay here with us?'

'For now, yes. In the long run, he might have to move to another home. We have a bed here, but it'll be taken in three weeks. Do you have any possessions with you, Andrew?'

'No, only my crazy get-up,' he said as he looked down at his garish garments.

'I'll have a look in lost property, see if there's anything that'll fit you and you can have that.'

'Thank you. Thank you so much, Jason!' Random clasped Jason's right hand and with a double clasp, shook it vigorously.

'Woah! Easy, that's quite a grip you've got there!'

'Sorry,' chuckled Random.

He released him and Jason rubbed his palm tenderly.

'Right, off to your rooms with all of you. But don't think you've escaped punishment, you two. You can wash the pots for a whole month and you're also grounded. Apart from school, I don't want you leaving this place for the next two weeks.'

'What about the Xbox?' Jake enquired hopefully.

'Definitely no Xbox for a fortnight, either.'

Crud! What'll I do now? Read! Pfft. Not likely.

'Go on then, off to your rooms, all of you. I'll get on to the council immediately, try and confirm Andrew's stay with us for the immediate future.'

'Thanks, Jason, thanks for everything,' said Anji sincerely.

The trio trudged off silently back to Anji's room. Closing the door behind them, they slumped to the floor and breathed a collective sigh of relief.

'I can't believe we've just got away with that,'

said Anji.

'It's tragic it really is. No computer games for a month,' muttered Jake, his face crestfallen.

'How did we do that, Random?' asked Anji.

'Simple. A simple manipulation of the truth.'

'I hate lying.'

'We didn't lie, Anji. We just didn't tell them the bits that could get us into real trouble.'

'We already are in real trouble!' insisted Jake. 'James is missing, our teacher's neck is on the line and we've probably got detention from now until we die!'

Random laughed to himself.

'When you've seen the trouble I've seen, Jake, you'd never think that you'll ever be in real trouble again.'

'Then why did you lie about your name?'

'Come on, do you really think I'd have got away with my story if I said that my name was Random? I had to come up with the first ordinary name I could think of.'

He stood up, took in a deep breath and smiled at his companions.

'So, now that's all sorted, let's do something fun instead.'

'Like what?' asked Anji.

Random grinned.

'Anything we like.'

VII

James Butcher had never been a brave boy. Whatever chromosome deployed the bravery gene in a person, it wasn't found anywhere in his genetic make-up. It was a trait that had been lacking somewhat throughout his family's history.

James was descended from a long-line of cowards, cheats, liars and swindlers. If, one day, he care look back on his family tree and pour back through the centuries, he would find that his great-great-great grandfather times twelve was in fact the Head Monk of the Augustinian Order who in 1532, in charge of the Holy Trinity Priory, became the first monastery that was dissolved by King Henry VIII.

Despite his pleas to keep the priory open, he eventually turned his back on his fellow monks and ran off before the place was torn down.

The cowardice got passed down to all generations and now, five hundred years after bravery was lost in the gene pool of the Butcher family, the latest generation was sat fixated in a trance on a spaceship he believed to be a film set, being menaced by a man made of sand.

But he was not alone in this mad, mad world.

There was a robot skateboard, who just to affirm that James' sanity was well and truly dwindling, spoke the Queen's English.

'You can't keep him here…' Skateboard paused, struggling to betray his etiquette protocols and finish his sentence with, 'Sir.'

'Don't tell me what to do you piece of sheet metal,' the Sandman hissed. 'The boy stays with us.'

Skateboard sighed.

'There are 7 billion inhabitants on this planet. You are only one entity and even then you're not all in one piece. He has done nothing wrong.'

'He has seen too much,' said the Sandman, more grains pouring from his form.

'Let me make a suggestion. Take me; I am a servant after all. Do what you want with me but leave him be.'

'Oh, don't you worry your little hydraulics about that, I will,' the Sandman had many ideas of the best way to torture his pet.

'If you let him go, then I shall give myself willingly over to you, but he cannot be used as a bargain chip. He is innocent.'

'Yes,' the Sandman was starting to see that having an earth boy on board didn't help him out whatsoever. He had read the same files as Skateboard had on the planet Earth.

Despite its primitive classification in the known universe, it was infamous for the home of the human race and they were equally as infamous for being a well-organised and occasionally aggressive race. Even with a ship as advanced as the Venus II, they couldn't take this world on alone.

Then, inside the Sandman's mind, a plan began to germinate.

'Okay, we'll play it your way, Skateboard. We'll let the boy go. Use your powers of persuasion to wipe his mind. Make him utterly convinced that this is a fantasy.'

I won't have any trouble doing that, thought Skateboard.

'He will lead us to Random.'

'Why do you want Random?'

The Sandman rounded on his slave. 'I've seen what's going on back on our home planet. Rodas is finding hope in what Random did. If I brought his head to the feet of Kalor Maloso then I can use his death to eventually take over the Crimson Empire and Rodas… and little by little, the universe will be mine!'

Anji looked anxiously over her shoulder.

'Quick!'

Jake plopped out of the tree and fell sharply onto his knee. He winced in pain as his kneecap cracked on the concrete pavement. Random helped him up to his feet almost instantaneously.

'You always knew how to make an entrance,' she chuckled.

'Where to now, my friends?' Random chirped.

The trio hatched their great plan as soon as Jason had left that evening for his romantic encounter with Miss Carter.

'Well, I predict that we have at least several hours before Jason gets back, so let's give you the grand tour,' Anji smiled.

Some of her old adventurous spirit had been stirred after their encounter with the police earlier so now she couldn't contain it. The thrill of sneaking out reminded her of the same rush she used to get when she stole from local newsagents. But she knew she'd never go back to her old life of crime. Sneaking out when grounded with her new alien friend would more than do for now.

They spent the next several hours visiting every tourist attraction Anji and Jake could think of. The Natural History Museum, the Science Museum, the British Museum and the Victoria and Albert Museum were all scrutinized with keen wonder by Random, who on the red bus away from Kensington Palace proclaimed that the Science Museum had been his favourite, especially the space section. He was particularly pleased that the trio were at one with a sea of ordinary people and no-one appeared to have even starred at them for more than three seconds!

The youngsters then embarked on Embankment, taking Random along the River Thames so he could observe the Houses of Parliament, the London Eye, Madame Tussauds and the Tower of London.

As the night drew in and the sun set on a wonderful day, Jake suggested that they walk around the Mall, down to Buckingham Palace and then finish their tour along the shops of Regent Street.

Before long, midnight was fast approaching and Anji had suggested that they get home before Jason arrived back. Tired and exhausted after their busy day, they arrived back at the children's home and with Random's superior strength coming in handy, were both carried to their beds by their new friend.

With a smile and a wave, he bid them good night, and retired to his new room.

After a few minutes of tossing and turning, Random snuggled cosily into his new blankets and fell into a deep, sweet sleep.

For the first day in his life, there had been no bloodshed. No horror.

Just fun.

It was the best day of his life.

VIII

Random was awoken sharply by a rasping knock at the door.

He rubbed his eyes and searched his new room for the time.

08:53.

He didn't know whether 08:53 was early or late, but for a Sunday, the seventh and last day of the week on the Earth, it felt far too early to be woken up!

'Come in.'

Jason walked through the doorway, struggling with a tray of food for the new child in care.

'Here we are. I wasn't sure what you liked so I thought I'd make you scrambled egg on toast along with a glass of orange juice.'

Random sat up in his new bed.

'Thanks, I've only ever had toast before. Where do eggs come from?'

Jason was taken aback by the question.

'Well…these eggs come from chickens.'

'Oh right, okay,' said Random. 'And the orange juice?'

Jason furrowed his brow. Was this kid taking the mickey?

'From oranges.'

'But I thought orange was a colour?'

'It is,' Jason replied.

'Then where did these oranges get their name from then?'

'From the colour.'

'Oh,' said Random puzzled, as he devoured a slice of toast. 'How odd.'

'I don't want to sound rude but have you ever been to school?'

'What's school?'

Jason let out a nervous laugh.

'Okay, that answers that question then. But how come you have learned to talk? And spell? And write?'

'By listening to others.' A fleck of scrambled egg clung onto the corner of Random's mouth like an unsightly zit.

'If only my schooling had been that simple. Speaking of which, did I tell you that I enrolled you in the same class as Jake and Anji. I presume you're the same age as them?'

'Yes, I presume so too,' lied Random.

'And no, you didn't tell me that you'd enrolled me at school.' Random's blood ran a little cold.

'Are you okay?' asked Jason.

'Yeah…just…nervous, I guess.'

Jason smiled.

'You'll be fine. If you need anything at all then I'll be downstairs. I'll introduce you to the other kids later on.'

He left and closed the door after him.

Random's appetite had completely gone.

'School!'

'It's worse than prison,' said Jake.

'Jake. It's not that bad,' Anji reassured. 'Plus you've never been to prison.'

'How do you know? I could have a really dodgy past?'

'Guys, please. You're not helping,' Random was rocking back and forth.

'This is ridiculous. I've taken on an entire army…TWO…to be precise. Spoken back to a cruel emperor and outrun those who want to kill me. I've piloted a spaceship to another world and yet I'm frightened of going to school!'

'You'll be fantastic!'

'But I'm so…thick! Your friend just had to tell me where the name of one of your fruits comes from?'

'Which one?' asked Jake.

'Oranges.'

'Where does it come from then?'

'The colour.'

'Oh…I never knew that. You see, you're already more intelligent than me. And you've never been to school.'

'Doesn't say much for your education system then!' smiled Random.

'Hey!'

'He's got a point,' laughed Anji. 'Seriously Random, you'll be fantastic. I promise you.'

Random got up and walked over to Anji's computer.

'Perhaps I should give myself a head start.'

'What do you mean?' asked Anji.

'Remember that technology section in the Science Museum we went to yesterday? They mentioned something called "the internet."'

Random pulled the desk chair away and looked for the power button.

'If my memory serves me correct, and my memory is flawless, I should be able to use your computer to learn everything I need to know.'

'Pfft. That'll take you ages,' dismissed Jake.

'No it won't,' smiled Random.

With lightning speed, he shot through the complete history of everything, including: the origins of man, the scientific theories that had shaped the world to its modern formation, the very basis of humanity and mathematical equations. It was all at his disposal.

You name it, he read it. He even found time to memorise the starting line-ups for the 1985 FA Cup final.

He read and assimilated it into his mind and in just under four minutes every minute detail was now stored in his incredible brain.

'Finished!'

With glee, he looked away from the monitor and stared at his watching friends. Their expressions bore a look of utter astonishment not too dissimilar from the one they wore when they witnessed the Venus II crash land just two days earlier.

'Wow…what level do you read at?' asked Anji.

'Supersonic level,' he gleamed back.

Suddenly, he noticed a strange burning sensation coming from under his nose. Looking down, the keyboard lay simmering in smoke.

Random turned to Anji.

'Sorry.'

'It doesn't matter,' said Jake, tearing away to his bedroom, 'let's see how fast you can do my homework!'

*

James Butcher awoke with a murmur next to a familiar looking pond. Rubbing his head, he groggily got to his feet and stared all around him. Had what he seen really happened?

It all seemed so real to him; the man made of sand, the spaceship, the polite robot. Where had they all gone? Were they all just figments of his imagination? He had too many questions to ask and no one around to answer them since he stood alone in the vibrant woodland.

'What a dream!' he sighed as he made for the woods edge.

He had no concept that he had been missing for a day. It felt like only a few minutes had passed since he had gone…wherever he had gone. Only it wasn't.

In the far distance, he could hear the sound of footsteps in the undergrowth. A moment later, he picked up the sound of dogs barking, their strained tones coming ever closer.

'Hello? Miss Carter?'

James walked towards the noises and closer to safety. As he did, he could feel invisible eyes burning on the back of his neck.

He didn't feel like he really was all alone.

*

Safe within the bowels of the Venus II, Skateboard watched on helplessly as the last possible comrade at his side walked off to safety. He would only hope that the memory blocker he had been forced to impose on the young boy would, as he had instructed, stop working after twelve hours.

That should give him enough time to find Sir and notify him of the situation.

'Don't you dare underestimate my intelligence again, you worthless piece of junk,' the Sandman was resting on the pilot's seat, his arm dribbling away.

'You've forsaken me before and it won't happen again. Will it?'

'No…Sir,' Skateboard conceded. His circuitry was wired up to short circuit if he was disobedient again. He had to do this, the Sandman ordered it. He didn't want his sand getting into his motherboard and corrupting it. That could kill him. He was truly the servant now to an unwanted master.

'Keep tracking the boy. He'll lead me to Random and my future glory!'

Skateboard sighed and slugged off to the control unit.

Silently, the Venus II left the woods and returned to the city.

IX

'Right class, settle down now. Lucy! Sit down will you!'

Lucy Paxman couldn't stop looking at the new boy in class. When she clasped eyes on him, time seemed to stop. Everything else just seemed to melt away. She had never seen anyone as beautiful as the handsome, purple boy in front of her. Mrs Henderson snapped her out of her trance.

'Sorry, Miss,' Lucy blushed as she rushed to her chair.

'I think you're in there, mate!' nudged Jake.

Random knew about the concept of attraction. But it did nothing for him. Love was not something he was interested in right now, especially as he was doing his best to blend in with his peers, which was rather difficult when his skin was as purple as an embarassed beetroot.

Noisily, the students scrapped their chairs against the cold floor of the classroom and fell silent.

'Thank you. Now then, we have a new pupil here at St Thomas. Would you like to introduce yourself, Andrew?'

Random gulped.

'Yes, sure.'

He pushed himself away from the wooden desk and walked to the front of the class.

Feeling the gaze of dozens of his new classmates on his back, he began to blush.

'Now, we normally play a game with our new students,' said Mrs Henderson, her straight brown locks flowing down her pleasant, smiling face. 'We call it high five. It's a technique that we use to get to know one another. You can choose any student at random. Is that okay?'

'Of course,' smiled Random.

'Has anybody got a question for Andrew?'
A sea of hands shot into the air. Everyone put their hands up, except Anji, who looked on with a mixture of worry and amusement.

'Blimey, there are quite a few of you. Right fire away,' said Mrs Henderson.

'Before we start, how many of you are only putting your hands up because you'd like to know if I'm an alien or not?'

The children shot sheepish looks at one another. A murmur gathered like a fog around the classroom.

'Or about the fact that I'm purple skinned?'

The same uncomfortable air hung all around.

'Well, I'll save you the time. No, I'm not an alien. And my skin colour is due to an unfortunate birthmark. Does that answer your questions?'

Two-thirds of the audience brought their arms neatly down by their sides again.

Lucy left her arm up.

'Are you purple all over?' she squeaked, playing with her hair as she spoke.

'That'll be enough of that!' said Mrs Henderson.

Random blushed. He'd have to watch out for that one!

Random survived an otherwise benign scrutiny of his character. Cautiously answering every question with the skill of a politician, he circumvented those who queried his past.

As before, it was only a matter of leaving some of the details out. No lies were told, just a manipulation of the truth.

His first lesson of the day was Maths and it was the first time that he had been separated by Jake and Anji.

The first thing that Random had received when he arrived at the school was his timetable. He was rather shocked to learn that he was only in one class with Anji, which was Art, and two with Jake, which were Home Economics and English.

As he took his place in the old Maths room, he sighed. He'd learnt every single mathematical equation inside out on his internet search just a couple of days previously.

He now realised that blending in wasn't going to be the hardest part of his day. It was going to be staying awake!

Random sat alone at the front of the classroom. He had suffered nothing but funny looks from the students at St Thomas all morning. He couldn't work out whether they were frightened of him or whether they were simply trying to work him out, but he didn't appreciate the attention. Especially from Lucy Paxman!

'Is anyone sitting here?'

Random looked up. It was her.

'Unfortunately not.'

'Cheeky!' Lucy laughed. 'Come on, scooch up!'

Random pulled his chair further over to the left-hand side of the desk and allowed Lucy next to him.

'I'm Lucy by the way.' She held out her hand.

'Hi Lucy,' Random deployed his unusual method of shaking hands again.

'You're a funny one aren't you! And cute too.'

Cute! Oh dear…

Random was starting to feel a little awkward.

'Do you have a girlfriend?'

'No.'

'Do you want a girlfriend?'

'Not right now, thanks.'

Lucy smiled. 'Playing hard to get are we?'

'Yes,' said Random curtly.

'Well, I love a challenge me. I always get my way eventually.'

Lucy smiled again. Random could not ignore her pretty features: Milky skin, blonde hair in bunches and a smile that could open the lock to the Headmaster's drinks cabinet.

'I'm sure,' Random retorted. Slowly, he softened. 'Look I think you're a very attractive girl, but to tell you the truth I'm only interested in friendship for now.'

Lucy's smile wavered a little.

'I see.'

He held his hand out again and shook her hand in the conventional human way for a change.

'It's a pleasure to meet you, Lucy,' he smiled.

Lucy went red. She had only just clapped eyes on this stranger an hour earlier but already she was smitten. His brown hair was thick and wavy; his eyes a shade of bluey/red she had never, ever seen before. She'd dated most of the boys in her year but only because she was bored.

This boy was a challenge; a challenge she was willing to accept.

Each lesson, or period as the children called it, which confused Random beyond words, lasted an hour.

After forty seven minutes into his first experience of English schooling, he finally succumbed to the descending wave of sleep that had been brought about by the tedium of fractions.

'A late night, was it, Andrew?' snapped Mr Johnson.

Random snorted as he stirred.

'Sorry?'

'Well, I hope it was something important that means you're missing out on my lesson!'

Random looked at his tormentor. Mr Johnson was in his mid-fifties, balding and stood diminutively against the giant white board. In his thirty years as a secondary school teacher, he had built a reputation as a stern teacher; cruel, calculated and unforgiving. Math suited him down to a tee.

If he caught a student not paying attention he had a technique to show them up and teach them a lesson in concentration and appreciation of his art.

'Stand up, will you?'

Random did as he was told.

'Come over here.'

Random obeyed.

'If you're such an expert at fractions then I want you to finish the exercises on this board with no mistakes. If you do make a mistake, then it's lunchtime detention for you. Do you understand?'

'I don't think I can,' replied Random.

'Why not?'

'Well, you've managed to rub most of the fractions off with your hand.'

Mr Johnson froze. His class began to chuckle softly.

He looked down to the flat edge of his left hand. An inky blur of what was once a taxing sequence of equations stained his skin.

A vein began to throb visibly under his ear. Quickly, he wrote the equations up again.

'Right, think you're so smart, do you? Try these ones for size!' Mr Johnson barked, spittle falling from his mouth like a dog.

Lucy's mouth dropped. She had never seen someone take Mr Johnson on like this before. For years, Mr Johnson had maintained the title of 'Scariest Teacher in the Whole School.'

His temperament and no-nonsense approach was the stuff of legend. Stories of his public dressing-down to crying children gained mythical status and the surrounding primary schools were full of kids who had heard all about him.

By the time they grew older and joined St Thomas, they all preyed that they would never be so unlucky as to have him as a teacher. Yet here he was, taken to task by a new boy!

'Fine.'

With lightning quick movements, he snatched the pen out of Mr Johnson's clammy hand and instantly proceeded to complete the series of fractions and equations with the ease of a Maths professor.

The class looked on in utter surprise.

In just eight seconds, Random had completed the complex sequence of equations. He lent up against the white board and crossed his arms in cocky defiance.

'By the way, you'll notice that with question eleven I made an amendment. Your question was flawed. In order to get to the answer you wanted, I had to carry the three and that was impossible with the equation you'd drawn up.'

Mr Johnson looked at him like an angry fish. His mouth dropped to the floor whilst his eyes bulged. He had been shown up. For the first time in his life, a young student had beaten him at his own game.

'Was there anything else?' Random grinned as he made his way back to his desk. The classroom erupted in a chorus of cheers and applause.

Random caught Lucy's gaze as he sat down.

So, this is what real love feels like, she thought.

*

'What do you mean there is nothing you can do!'

Mr Johnson slammed his fist onto the headmaster's desk. Mrs Anderson, who had presided over the school for forty years, sat defiantly behind her desk.

'The little swine humiliated me! Me! I mean, come on.'

He slumped into the chair next to Random, who was trying to be as quietly smug as possible.

'In what way did you humiliate Mr Johnson?' the headmaster enquired.

'I completed his sums on the board just as he asked,' said Random.

'Is this what happened?'

Mr Johnson's veins were throbbing like mad under his thin skin.

'Yes, but...' he fiddled with the thin tufts of hair twirling on his flat head, 'it was the manner in which he conducted himself. He was all, "oh, I had to carry the three because you're such an incompetent man that you had to write all the equations back up on the board as you keep rubbing it off". I can't be expected to do anything right, nowadays, can I!'

Mrs Anderson raised her hand in an attempt to sooth the flustered Maths teacher.

'Now, Charles, I have to stop you there. I don't think the boy needs to hear you go any further. I suggest you go back to your classroom and relax. You do have a free period, after all.'

Mr Johnson sighed and bowed his head in defeat. 'Very well.' His sweaty palms left a mark on the table as he left the room, glaring at Random as he departed.

'Are they all like this?' Random enquired. 'I mean, this is my first lesson here at this school and I'm already in the headmaster's office. If this is what school is like then how will I ever learn anything?'

Mrs Anderson smiled. 'Don't you worry about old Mr Johnson. He has had a rough time of late and judging by the speed and accuracy of your sums on the whiteboard, I'd say that ten minutes out of your time in the classroom will not harm your learning here at St Thomas.'

Random nodded in agreement.

'Apart from all of that, how are you settling in?' asked Mrs Anderson.

'I've not really had a chance to get my feet under the desk yet. They keep changing with every lesson. I don't think I have my own desk, do I?'

The Headmaster shook her head slightly, trying to displace the rather complex response.

'Anyway, if you need anything, my door is always open.'

Random was muddled by this. He remembered distinctively that the door was firmly closed when Mr Johnson had marched him over to her office. Believing this to be a one-off and not just a turn of phrase, he happily got up from his chair and left. He dug into his inside pocket and fished around for his timetable.

'PE. Whatever that is. Oh joy!'

In a lifetime of uncertainty, at least Random had settled upon one conclusion.

Student life sure was confusing!

X

'How is it going, Andrew?'

Random recognised the all too flippant tones of Jake like he had known him all his life.

The Rodasian groaned into his hands.

'This isn't going very well?'

'What's wrong?' asked Anji. The pair looked down at their purple friend, who was lying prostrate on one of the few picnic benches that scattered the lively playground.

'Being a student is the worst. I could safely say that I'd prefer to be chased by a knife wielding Kalor Maloso down a dark alley than come here again.'

'Let me guess, culture shock?' enquired Jake.

'Do you know how many times I have been asked if I am an alien? Actually, I'll tell you; 37 times. In the first hour I sent one teacher suffering from a mid-life crisis into meltdown, gained a stalker and set fire to the frog we were dissecting in Biology.

'How on earth....?' Jake didn't have time to finish his question.

'AND the teacher...and the desk...in the end I got sent back to the classroom and had to read a pamphlet someone had left lying around called,

"Fire! The do's and do nots of fire safety." It was adorned by a crude illustration of a character called Fiona the Firefly.'

'Ah yes, we had the local fire services come over the other week and give us a talk,' said Anji.

The teacher compared me to a student he had called Simon Dudley.

'Oh, yes! I used to like him. Whatever happened to him?' wondered Jake.

'He set fire to the Headmaster's cat,' replied Anji.

'Ah.'

Random groaned again and rolled onto his side.

Anji jabbed Random's arm. 'Well, at least PE must have been fun.'

He peeked through his purple digits, as if to hide himself from a waking nightmare.

'Fun? FUN!'

'I'll take that as a no, then.' Anji's smile wavered.

'I walked to the gym and was told that there were no new kits available. So whilst the school was waiting on new kits to arrive, I would have to wear lost property. Have you ever worn lost property clothes before? It stank! The top I wore was far too small and looked like a boob tube!

The underarms stank worse than a planet of farts. The less said about the shorts the better.

Despite being far too big, I somehow managed to tie them around my waist, but I looked like I was wearing a kilt! The stench meant that during Rugby practice nobody dared mark me in case the biological warfare emitting from my person was contagious. One boy wretched in his own mouth and was sick when he was tackled.'

Jake pointed his finger in the air to make an injunction.

'And what's more.'

He slowly lowered it again.

'When the ball - and let me tell you if that is what a ball looks like on this planet then the Earth is a rhombus - came to me and I was encouraged to kick it, I pelted it with such force that it bent the post all the way back, knocked out the teaching assistant and the "ball" kept going.'

'Well,' Anji was clutching at straws. 'Where did the ball go?'

'Who knows...Kent, probably!,' replied Random curtly.

'Who's the stalker?' asked Jake, although he dare enquire at this point.

'Over there.'

Random pointed to the other side of the table, which was a mere three feet away. There sat Lucy, waving and blushing like the adoring fan she was.

Random waved meekly back, whilst Anji did

her best to stifle a laugh.

'It's no laughing matter!' cried Random. 'Do you know what this means? It means that I've done exactly what I didn't want to do. I've drawn attention to myself.'

Anji nodded. 'This hasn't gone to plan, has it?'

'Not by any stretch of the imagination,' Random confirmed.

Unbeknownst to the trio, a figure was walking up from behind, his pace gathering as he got closer. Random lay on his back and shielded the sun from his eyes. Soon afterwards, a shadow loomed over him, blotting the warm ray out completely.

'James!' cried Jake.

Random opened his eyes and looked up to find the bewildered face of a teenage boy towering above him.

He licked his lips, his mouth dry and cracked.

'Are you the one who they found in the woods?'

Random nodded enthusiastically. If James were here, maybe Skateboard and the Venus II were close by also.

'How did you get back here?' asked Anji.

James ignored her question and continued to stare at Random and Random alone.

'I think we need to have a chat.'

Jake, Anji and Random led James under the

shelter of a tree into a more secluded area of the playing field. Their party had almost been joined by a fifth member, but Lucy was warded off by Random, who suggested to his "fan" that she might want to spend time with Jake instead. She shook her head, disgusted and left them alone, leaving Jake's ego severely dented.

Random sat James down and sat cross legged next to him.

'Tell me everything,' he cooed, his voice quiet, almost like a whisper.

'I saw the ship crash land before me.'

'We didn't see anyone at the pond, where were you?' said Jake. Suddenly, the boy remembered the conversation he had with Anji moments before the crash. 'Hang on a minute, what did you hear?'

'I wasn't prying or anything, honest,' said James. He had always been a little afraid of Jake. Not that the teenager was a bully, but James had been the unfortunate recipient of a cruel lunchroom prank that Jake had played. James was known throughout the year as the "swot", the one whose homework was in on time, all the time, and the first to put his hand up when answering a question in class.

Jake, feeling slighted by the adoration James deservedly received from his teachers, decided to spike his ham and cucumber sandwich with cheese. A fairly innocuous act, many would think, but not when the person being fooled was lactose intolerant.

To make matters worse, Jake had chosen the one day in the week, nay the entire school year, that James had forgotten his epi-pen.

Two days in hospital and a month's worth of detentions later, James and Jake were hardly what you would call 'friends.'

'I didn't hear anything, honest!' screamed James, afraid that his chief tormentor would do something terrible to him again. 'I couldn't hear a thing…apart from the engine roar that is. I thought I had wandered onto a film set! So, while it was smoky and nobody could see me, I wandered on board. Then I saw both you and your purple friend here follow me in. I didn't want to reveal myself since, well; we aren't particularly friends are we?'

Jake turned his head, confirming James' suspicions.

'Anyway, all of sudden, you lot were gone and I was left by myself. The ship was rocking and I was lost in what looked like the engine bay. By the time I came back to the entrance, it was closed and I found this talking metal robot.

'Skateboard!' squealed Random. 'Is he okay?'

'I think so. It all seemed such a blur. I was convinced, in fact, I was absolutely 100% certain that I was on a film set. It all looked so convincing. Like something out of *Star Wars* or *Doctor Who*. I wanted to meet the stars.'

'That's all very well, but how did you get back here, James?' asked Anji.

James searched his memory.

'Never mind that!' interrupted Random. 'Where is Skateboard now?' Now he thought of it, the past two days had been almost unbearable for Random. He was a stranger in a strange land, a misfit of the stars grounded to an alien plain that he didn't belong to. Skateboard was his constant. He had escaped Rodas with him. And then he was lost. Abandoned almost. Knowing that Skateboard was nearby filled Random's heart with pure unadulterated joy.

'I'm not sure. I'm sorry.'

Random's heart ceased to flutter and he sagged despondently.

'You're alien aren't you? None of it was make-believe was it?' James enquired.

Random, fed up with the lies he had been telling all day, nodded his head.

'Yes, but you can't tell anyone, James. Not a word. We need to keep it between us. Do you understand?' Anji clasped James' arm, hoping for his co-operation.

'I do, although I don't understand any of this and I definitely do not want to be part of it.'

'I understand,' said Anji. 'Do you know what happened next?'

'I don't really know. It's really foggy. I remember talking to the robot and then...there was someone else there.'

Random looked up, his face a picture of concern.

'Who was it?' asked Jake.

'I don't know. He looked injured. Badly injured in fact and from what I remember, I don't think he was all there.'

Random scrambled to James's side and grabbed hold of James desperately, his hands like pincers.

'What do you mean, "I don't think he was all there?"'

James was taken aback by Random's actions. He tried to speak but he could see the wild panic in Random's eyes. The red and blue iris danced in a pool of fear.

'I...I...I don't know.'

'Try, for deqes sake!' swore Random.

'Random take it easy,' said Anji. Both she and Jake's hearts were pounding. Something had made Random angry and frightened it seemed.

'He kept...leaking,'

'Leaking...' Random repeated, tiny beads of sweat emitting from the pores on his brow.

'Yeah, he was just...dripping away; flaking

like sand in an egg timer.'

'Sand...' repeated Jake.

'Yes...' said James. 'That's it. Now I remember...'

Random, Anji and Jake dared not breathe.

'It was a man made of sand...'

*

Skateboard felt different. It was a feeling he hadn't felt before, like there was a restriction to certain file paths in his circuits. A strange air of obedience filled his metal mind. Never in his lifetime, since his motherboard was first activated, had he felt more peculiar.

Every AI robot constructed in the cybernetics division of the Sapphire Regime was implemented with a compliancy chip. Its job was to keep the AI in line with its master and maintain quality standards when sold to its customers.

Somehow, on the day that Skateboard was assembled, his compliancy chip was not so much corrupted, but something had slipped in his programming.

Under normal circumstances, at the quality check, this would have been highlighted by the final diagnostics run by the technicians at the plant.

But for Skateboard, he was allowed to leave the production line and go out into the world of chaos for active service; and that world of chaos was Rodas.

His creators had failed to discover that what they had done was created an AI with free will.

Skateboard's recent memories faded in and out of his metal head.

'Didn't you know that you had the greatest gift anyone in the universe can be given? How stupid you must have been to never know.'

There it was; that maniacal voice of the Sandman coursing through his mind. How could his worst enemy have known something he had failed to discover about his own being before he had?

'What are you doing…inside my thought patterns?'

'You don't remember? I infiltrated you. I couldn't have you running off again. You're far too important to me for that; you and that boy.'

'I told you I would comply.' Skateboard was having trouble speaking. His could feel parts of him corrupting.

'Better to be safe than sorry. What do you do when your pet runs away? Make sure you keep them on a lead at all times.'

It was impossible for a robot to feel pain, but Skateboard was starting to feel shooting sparks of torment around his motherboard.

'But...my security protocols.'

'Bypassed. After all, it only took a grain of sand to get in. Damn stuff gets everywhere. Wouldn't you agree?'

Skateboard screamed in agony. His entire body started convulsing as tiny blue charges imploded under his chassis.

'Please. Get out of me.' The robot started to yelp. His body was being violated and there was nothing he could do to stop it.

To escape such a degrading experience, he would have to do the one thing he despised more than anything else. He would have to beg.

'Please...please, you're torturing me!'

'I can see all of you. This is...incredible!' The Sandman chuckled.

'W-w-what...are you...going to...do to me?'

'I can be in two places at once. As my physical form dwindles, I can inhabit yours. You're right, you know? There's no way that I can take on Random alone. But now, there are two of us.'

Skateboard delved hard in his circuitry, trying to fight the overwhelming might of the Sandman.

'What are you doing?'

The Sandman could feel his victim reaching for something deep down in his being, something an AI must only turn to in emergencies such as this.

'No! You wouldn't dare!'

'I would; I would do anything to stop you from hurting these people!'

The Sandman erupted into a guttural laughter.

'If you self-destructed, you'd blow up this ship. You'd strand your friend on this primitive planet. You'd condemn him to a life trapped here. Actually it isn't such a bad idea.'

Skateboard strained with what was left of his willpower.

'What?'

'Well, I'll be alright; I'll just be blown into atoms. Don't worry, I can rebuild again. Maybe I could inhabit humans too? Shame I hadn't thought of that before, I'd have taken over that boy…oh, wait a minute. That's right…I already have…'

The boy! How could he?

'You are a sick man, Sandman,' he struggled.

'Oh, hadn't you noticed,' the Sandman smiled. His essence burrowed deeper into the core of Skateboard's motherboard. All his circuits were corrupting now. The fight was nearly over.

Try as he might, Skateboard just couldn't do it. His will was snapped, encompassed by evil. His self-destruct switch unreachable by sheer force of will, Skateboard succumbed to the inevitable.

And then, there was darkness.

*

In an instant, James's eyes snapped shut and his head bowed to the ground. Random shook the boy vigorously.

'James…James, come on wake up!'

'What happened?' asked Anji.

'It looks like someone's just shut him off,' said Jake.

'Oh no! Jake's right, I think they have,' concluded Random.

'How?' asked Jake.

'If James has been in contact with the Sandman…' Random's sentence tailed off, allowing his brain to catch up with his mouth. '…then there is the slightest possibility that he has been infiltrated by him.'

'Sounds disgusting,' said Anji.

'This really isn't a laughing matter. Think about it. What do you always bring back from the beach with you?'

'Sea shells?'

'Try again. I'll give you a clue; flakes of grains stuck in the gaps between your toes.'

'Sand!' exclaimed Anji. 'It always gets stuck to your body.'

'Precisely. You remember what he said. If the Sandman really is falling apart, then it would be easier to get bits of the grains that make up his body on your person. The Sandman is a powerful being. He was an experiment to turn a normal man into an ultimate warrior, however, this experiment went wrong. He has got the capability to do anything.'

'Even control a person,' Jake said seriously.

In a flash, James lifted his head and his eyes snapped open. Anji and Jake jumped but Random was unmoved. The boy cracked his right fist square into the jaw of the Rodasian and sent Random tumbling backwards.

Anji screamed as James leapt onto Random's reeling body and clasped his hands around his neck.

'Come on!' Jake pulled Anji. The teenagers tried with all their might to pull James' possessed weight off Random.

The alien started choking, his windpipe crushed from the weight of the boy that loomed over him.

As he started blacking out, Random looked up at his attacker and stared into his eyes.

They were a deep tone of beige. James was no longer a slightly annoying earthling from the suburbs of London. He was the Sandman.

XI

It took a herculean effort, even for someone with the might that Random possessed. The alien stopped grappling at James' strangling hands and concentrated on his arms instead.

He blinked through the pain barrier and saw his two companions grappling at the boy but to no avail. For all the hitting, slapping, punching and scratching, both were ineffective.

'I'm sorry to do this James,' choked Random. With one swift movement he karate chopped James' left arm. The limb bent to a peculiar angle and a sickening crack emitted from within. James showed no pain; no expression of anguish cracked on his emotionless face.

Random emerged from underneath and flipped James onto his back, pinning his arms down by his side and head butting his attacker unconscious, or so he thought.

'Rope…now!' he barked, his vocal chords constricted by the pressure of his almost collapsed wind pipe.

Jake and Anji were shocked by what they had just seen, but they hurried to their feet and made off for the playground.

A twisted smile emerged on the bloodied lips of Random's attacker.

'You think violence will stop me?' tutted "James".

'Why don't you come out here and face me properly, you coward!' screamed Random. Although they were well covered by the woodland and the schoolchildren were quite a distance away from the fight, Random was still cautious of being discovered but his emotions were starting to get the better of him.

'Oh…just you wait.' James tones were full of malice.

'Leave him alone! I don't want to hurt him. He hasn't done anything wrong.' Random picked "James" up by the scruff of his shirt. 'You leave his body and I'll come quietly.'

'You want to protect the innocent, do you?' James was starting to sound more and more like the Sandman by the second. He started laughing again.

'Oh Random, you can keep punching me until this body I have inhabited becomes nothing more than a bloodied pulp, but you won't will you? That is where people like you and me differ. I'll do anything to obtain my goal. I would burn down this city and all its pitiful inhabitants if it meant my inner peace and freedom, but you? You favour diplomacy. It'll get you nowhere.'

'What do you mean?' said Random.

'We are far beyond negotiation. You betrayed

me once. I can never let that go. I will NEVER let you go. You left me on that planet of pain and suffering but you couldn't escape me. You'll never escape me. I will not rest until you are crushed into dust. Let's see how you like it.'

"James" smiled again. Malevolence oozed from his lips. Random had heard enough. He dropped his attacker to the ground and did nothing as the Sandman began to chuckle to himself.

As Jake and Anji raced back toward the woodland, accompanied with rope procured from the gym cupboard, a laugh, so dark and evil the clouds seemed to thicken above them, echoed in the air.

Anji glanced over to her friend as her breathing grew heavier. Both of them wore a look of severe concern.

'Anj…' Jake wheezed. 'What are we going to do?'

*

The Sandman had propped himself up in the pilot's chair in the Venus II. With his eyes closed, he could easily have been mistaken for being asleep by a passer-by, but a trance state seemed to pass over his failing body.

Skateboard whirred into the cockpit and took up

residency next to his master.

The Sandman awoke, almost as though he could feel his metal subject's presence.

'Contact has been made.'

'I know; I felt it, my master.' Skateboard's tones were different now that he had given in to the Sandman's will. They were darker, calmer than before and more in tune with his masters own voice.

The Sandman tried to get up but staggered against the instrument panel. As he stuck his hand out to steady himself, more grains of sand tumbled to the floor.

'Master, you are weak. You should rest. You cannot sustain three bodies at once, especially in your state.'

'I know,' uttered the Sandman. He felt weary.

'I need…rejuvenation. Skateboard, suggestions?'

Skateboard's circuits whirred.

'There does not appear to be any organic matter in the area that will replenish your physical form. You need to be reconfigured as an entire entity.'

'I know, but I can't do that, can I? Half of me is back on Rodas.'

He fell back into the chair, panting from exhaustion.

'I'm being tortured across star systems,

Skateboard. Stretched among the stars. I feel…so much pain; pain that I cannot describe.' He hesitated. 'I dare not describe.'

Skateboard pondered on his new master's words.

'A suggestion, master; inhabit yourself within the ship fully?'

'I can't. I'd burn up. In all honesty, I'm on fire right now. Aflame in four different places at once. Your AI system is easy to corrupt, even for a simple solider like me. But a whole ship?' he shook his head. 'It would kill me.'

'Another suggestion, master; on this planet, there is a similar substance to that in which your physical form was mutated. It will not yield your pain but it will restore your physical form temporarily. However, you'd have to act quickly.'

'Skateboard?' the Sandman whispered. 'Is there any way in which I can be one again?'

'None, I'm afraid, master.'

The Sandman let out a little yelp.

'Is that a death sentence you've just given me?'

'Yes,' said Skateboard, coldly.

Blobs of water droplets started leaking out of the corners of the Sandman's eyes, collating in clumps of sand on his cheeks.

'I don't fear it. A soldier never fears death. I'll embrace it when it comes'. He sniffed. 'If it is death that beckons me near, then I am taking that boy to hell with me. I want to make him watch how much it burns. The horror of it all. In his final seconds…then he'll understand.'

With renewed vigour, the Sandman limped out of the chair.

'Find me a new body. Now!'

It was the smile that perturbed Anji the most. Not the fact that a boy from her year was acting as an unwilling and unknowing host for an alien body, but horrific formation of his lips sprouting from the gag that the trio had improvised out of Jake's school tie.

'How did this happen?'

Random sat on the floor and stared into nothingness.

'The Sandman has become desperate. He knows he cannot face me in his current state. It sounds like the majority of him is still back home.'

'But if he is made of sand then how can he control and feel?' Jake asked.

'Good question,' said Anji.

'The molecules that made up his humanoid body were corrupted but it doesn't mean he still can't feel. Or think. But imagine this. You're pulled between here, there, everywhere. Literally! It's bad enough if you pull a muscle. Imagine being stretched across planets.'

'I'd rather not,' said Jake. 'What's the plan?'

Random looked at his friend. In the same moment, the lunch bell rang.

'Well, we can't go back to our classes, not now, 'said Anji.

'We'll be done for truanting! We are in enough trouble with Jason as it is!' pointed out Jake.

'Well, what else do you suggest?'

'No, Jake's right, you two should go back to class.'

Anji and Jake looked at Random in astonishment.

'No, we are not leaving you,' cooed Anji.

'Anji, you are dealing with matters that you can never understand,' Random picked up her hand and held it up to his chest. 'I understand the sentiment but I've got you two in enough trouble as it is and I'd never forgive myself if either of you got hurt.'

'Well, you're stuck with us,' said Jake. He put his hand on Random's shoulder.

'How sentimental,' spat "James" through his gag.

'Shut up, you!' shouted Anji.

Random marched over to the bound body of James, looked him square in the eye and removed the gag.

'You think words will hurt us? No, we'll fight fire with fire. So wherever you are, whatever you've done to Skateboard, I'm ready for you. You know where I am. You can have me. Meet me here tonight, the real you, I mean, and we'll end this. Bring Skateboard with you'.

'Don't I get to make terms?' choked the Sandman through James' voice.

'You get me…isn't that the best term you can think of?'

Nodding, "James" relented.

'Is there anything else while you're feeling brave?'

'You leave James alone right now. Leave him. Let the seed of evil dissolve and die. You don't need him anymore. Then, and only then, will I agree to meet you.'

"James" emitted another twisted smile.

'Random…tonight you will meet your maker at my hands…and I'll bathe in your blood.'

With a jolt, "James'" head tipped back against the tree he was tied to and he wretched an almost microscopic shard of sand out of his throat. Random traced it with his vision and saw it blow away in the cool breeze.

James coughed as Jake and Anji untied him.

'Welcome back to the land of the living,' smiled Random.

'What has happened...why am I...oh no! My arm! What have you done to my arm!?' James stared in horror at the bone jutting out of his flesh.

'Ah, this might take some explaining!' said Jake.

XII

'Out of my way!'

The Sandman had endured a multitude of horrors in his life. This included the battle of Karebas, being torn away from his family, mutated and ripped physically across galaxies. Now he could add one more horrific experience to his tally - rush hour in London.

Against Skateboard's advice, he decided it was a good idea to walk to the school where his possession of James had been such a success. Despite his frail form and the fact that so many people would see him, he went against the better judgment of his slave and decided to leave the Venus II on foot.

Moments after his essence had left the schoolboy, he started to formulate a plan in his head on how to bring down Random. With the school fifteen miles away from the ship's new hiding place on top of some grand old building called "Buckingham Palace", he managed to slip down the drain pipe and integrate with the gravel on the path, slithering away from any unwanted attention from the strange looking guards in the tall furry hats.

After slinking away to a quiet side street, he

assimilated his coarse skin to pigmentation close to that of a human and even managed to fabricate some clothes. But this left him more hollow inside than he had felt in a long time and a piercing cavity opened up in his chest. Weaker than ever, he had to do this alone, without the aid of his ship or his dominated robot.

He also had to build up the willpower and the mental strength to withstand anything that Random was prepared to throw at him. With his face contorted in agony, the Sandman went on. He did his best to brush past the crowds, knowing that it would be easier to inhabit as many people as possible but also mindful that this would destroy him for good.

Stumbling along, weaker than he had thought, he glanced up at a bus stop sign and decided to hail an oncoming big red bus.

'Stop please!'

The driver was too busy chatting to an attractive man and did not see their potential passenger. As the bus sped past, it generated a huge gust of wind, which tore through the Sandman like a knife through hot butter.

Indignantly, and hoping that no one had seen his plight; the Sandman reassembled himself and cursed the human race.

Although his trip was long and arduous, he started to appreciate the human capacity for ignorance. Not one fellow traveller acknowledged his existence. Indeed, not one of the passengers on the Central Line train even talked to one another, let alone smiled! He didn't want to be noticed, so on this occasion he was thankful that he seemed invisible to everyone.

Roughly two miles away from the school, the Sandman collapsed. Again, nobody seemed willing to stop and help him, even though there were dozens of commuters in the same street as he. Panting and sweating profusely, the Sandman look around in desperation. He felt the sweet embrace of death reaching out towards him. Shaking his head, he blinked it away, ignoring such a trivial matter as death. He had to reach the school. He had to kill Random. It was fast becoming the last thing he ever wanted to do. With a great effort, he staggered to his feet. Limping, he soldiered on for another half a mile.

Right in front of him was a construction site.

Relief began to pour through his coarse veins. Laughing to himself, he passed straight through the eight-foot-tall gates, ignored the safety signs and warnings that this was a hard hat area, and wandered straight underneath the metal girders and machinery.

'Hey! You can't be in here, mate!' bellowed a worker.

'Can't I?'

'Nah, pal.' Another construction worker approached him from the opposite angle. 'We're closing up for the day and you're in a restricted area.'

'I need help,' choked the Sandman.

'Yeah, well come back in eighteen months when the hospital's done, will yer. Now come on, we wanna be getting home now. Ain't you got a family to be getting back to as well?'

The Sandman sized up both men. One was in his early thirty's and well-built for a human. Good soldier material, back home, thought the cornered Rodasian.

The other had a more rotund, squat body shape, his balding grey locks signifying his advancing years.

'No, why, do you?'

The Sandman edged his way closer to a large pile of sand that was left in a huge quantity next to the cement mixer.

'As a matter of fact, yeah,' said the older worker. 'Come on, we can't leave until you have.'

The younger worker butted in. 'Come on, mate. You're trespassing. You don't want us getting the authorities involved, do ya?'

The Sandman felt the rough texture of the sand against the soles of his feet. He smiled manically. He needed to try his might. Why not practice on these two?

'The more the merrier.'

In a blink of an eye, the Sandman disappeared. His form dissipated, much to the astonishment of the workers.

'Steve? What the heck?'

The younger worker gazed in shock at his colleague.

All of a sudden, a shot of sand exploded from the ground and lifted high in the air, towering above its victims.

Both stood petrified at the huge wave of sand that threatened to engulf them.

'Run!' shouted the older worker. Both men accelerated as fast as their legs could carry them but before they could reach the gate, the wave was upon them.

As the older man fell to the floor as the wave came crashing down upon him. The wave seemed to wail like a banshee, shrieking as it engulfed the pair. The last thing the younger man saw wasn't his family like he had hoped on his final day on earth. It was the terrifying image of a man's face in the sand as he and his colleague perished in the tidal wave.

The crash was heard all around. Confused passers-by raced to the site but the tidal wave was gone. All that was left were the corpses of two men, both with sand pouring from their mouths and ears, impossibly drowned on dry land.

XIII

It had been one heck of a day, a heck of a day. Random lay awake on his bed, his focus fighting back any temptation to sleep, but on the Sandman and what was to come. He picked himself out of the comfortable blankets and walked over to the window. He looked up at the silent stars as they glittered in the bleak sky. Sighing to himself, he folded his arms and zoned out.

How do you defeat an enemy who can assemble himself together again? Even if he was falling apart, Random knew that this was a powerful foe that he had to take down, no matter what the cost. But how?

Quietly, he tip toed across the room and opened the door. Checking that the coast was clear, he slipped across the hallway to Anji's room. Turning the door knob with the subtle nature of a courteous burglar, he was stunned to find that Anji was also standing at her window wide awake.

'Can't sleep?' he whispered.

'Like there's any chance of that,' she replied, imploring him to close the door.

'Listen, Anji, I've been thinking about tonight. I need to leave as soon as possible…alone.'

'What? You think that you can take him on by yourself?'

'No, it isn't that. I'm endangering you all. He could be out there, right now, watching me; waiting for me to make a move.'

'Waiting for US to make a move,' Anji held Random's hand. It was cold and clammy. She looked into Random's eyes.

'I know it's dangerous, but you shouldn't be fighting him alone.'

'People could get hurt. People have already been hurt!' Random walked over to her desk and sat on the corner, his legs dangling off the floor.

'James will be okay. Besides, it got us out of detention for being late back to class, didn't it?'

'Lies, excuses, what am I turning you into?'

Anji looked down. 'Actually, Random, I think I've always been like this. Ever since my parents died I've had this…void…this lack of direction. Believe me, I used to be a lot worse than this.'

'No way! I dread to think,' he smiled but it didn't convince Anji that his mood has changed.

'When I downloaded all the information off the internet I saw the feats that mankind have achieved; the wonders of the world, the love, the compassion. Then I saw the hate and the centuries of conflict. It reminded me so much of my planet that I couldn't bear to read on. The point is that I know what the human race is capable of, good and bad. And right now, I don't think that the discovery of two aliens scrapping on your world would do you any good.'

'You're right there,' Anji agreed. 'So…you don't see yourself staying then?'

'No.'

'So you're going back to Rodas then?'

'Oh no! I want to explore the universe! Take a look at all the stars and the different galaxies. I want to see as many of them as I can.'

'But what about your people?'

Random stuttered. He remembered the refugees that he walked past on his home world. The hopelessness in their eyes, the fear, the pain.

'I will return one day but I'm not ready to be there right now. Although I did make a promise to myself that I will save them, when the time is right.'

'What a burden,' Anji said.

'Yup,' Random agreed. 'It's the reason I'm here. To make things better, even if it means sacrificing myself for the millions back at home. You can't blame me for wanting to have a little bit of fun before then, could you?'

'I guess not,' Anji smiled. 'What time are we heading back to the school?'

'Is there nothing I can do to stop you and Jake coming with me?'

'Nope.'

Random sighed although deep down he was relieved that he wouldn't have to face the Sandman alone. He would never admit it to his friends, but he was scared. Scared of not being able to stop his enemy and scared that he wouldn't be able to save Skateboard. He was also scared incase he managed to lose the Venus II for good.

'Alright, but you two need to do exactly as I say, okay?'

'Gotcha,' Anji felt the thrill of adventure spark inside her. This feeling of the unknown was more exhilarating than any stealing spree…or arson attack on her classmate's gym shorts.

'We leave as soon as possible. Is there a way that we can get a message to Jake without waking Jason?'

'Please, all that assimilation of the internet and you failed to look up texting?' Anji tutted. She produced her phone and started typing away on the touch screen.

'Tell him to meet us in here in five clicks, er, I mean minutes. We need to leave as soon as possible.'

'You've got a plan, then?'

'Yes…well…half a plan.'

Anji frowned. 'Oh, well that's better than having none at all.'

'The Sandman is literally falling apart. If I can keep him occupied, keep him focused on me then I can wear him out. His life force is already ebbing away. Whilst I'm doing that, you need to break into the Venus II. Don't worry, it'll be there and you'll know when.'

'But what about Skateboard?' asked Anji. 'He'll kill us before we even have the chance to get close to him.'

'The Sandman is using mind control on him but as he will be fully distracted by me, it'll mean that his hold over Skateboard will not be as strong. You need to convince him to help us. I'm sorry if that sounds dangerous but that's how it's got to be, if you are willing to help me. If he doesn't comply, then use this.'

Random handed Anji a magnet, small enough to fit into a small pocket.

'Really? You're serious?'

'Use it if all else fails. It'll scramble his circuits and in that time you can regain the Venus. How does that sound?'

'Peachy.'

A third voice entered the bedroom. Jake had been standing there all along, fully dressed and ready to help.

'Remind me to lock that door in future,' joked Anji.

'Oi!' smiled Jake. He put his right hand out in

front of him.

'Are you ready to kick some alien ass? No offence Random!'

Random smiled and put his hand on top of Jake's.

'Let's kick it.'

Anji did the same, suggesting that the trio were ready to take on the world.

Their moment of joy was short lived. Random's ultrasensitive hearing picked up on a low hum coming from outside. The hum grew louder and louder until the other two also heard its tone.

'Oh daxque! Get down!'

Random pulled his friends to the ground as a bolt of energy shot through the bedroom window and collided with the wall, exploding in a ball of fire and plaster, waking up the rest of the home with a startle.

Another bolt sizzled into the bedroom, exploding again, this time nearly taking out the entire room behind it. A child screamed in terror.

'Get everyone out!' ordered Random as Jake and Anji ducked their way past more missile fire. Jason came running up the stairs, but he was stopped by another explosion.

'Come on, everyone out.'

Half a dozen screaming and crying children came hurtling down the stairs. Jason made a mental head count so as to not miss anyone.

Miss Carter appeared at the foot of the stairs in her nighty.

'Get them out of the building!' Jason screamed above the sound of destruction. Anji and Jake tore into the hallway, carrying a child each.

'Is that everyone?' screamed Jason.

'Random…where's Random?' shouted Jake.

'Whose Random?' asked Jason. Another shot of fire fizzed past his ear, destroying the top of the stairwell.

'Andrew!' he exclaimed.

He lifted Jake and Anji down onto the lower half of the stairwell, which still survived.

'Jason, come on jump!' implored Anji.

'I need to get Andrew first.'

'No, you need to get out the building, now!' hollered Jake.

The building was on fire. The roof groaned and splintered.

'Get out, quick!'

Jake and Anji's path to get to the front door was clear. Helplessly, they tore themselves away from the stairwell, carrying the two small children in their arms, and fled the burning home.

When they got outside, Miss Carter was gathering the children together, doing her best to console them all. Neighbours had poured out onto the street and were starting to help take the children away to safety.

'Where's Jason?' Miss Carter turned to Anji and shook her violently. 'Where is he?'

A loud crack interrupted her desperate pleas. As they watched on, the roof of the building, aflame with the red hot flames from the laser fire, caved in and splintered into the top floor.

Miss Carter screamed a scream that turned the air cold.

Random and Jason were still inside.

XIV

Random awoke and shook his head. His last memory was following Jake and Anji out of the bedroom. He lay on the burning ground, his clothes singed from the flames all around him. He looked down at the splintered wood from the beams that had previously held the roof together. He must have been knocked out by the falling shower.

He squeezed himself past the flames that blocked his passage out of the room. The air felt hotter than he had ever experienced in his life and it was becoming difficult to breathe. Clouds of black smoke plumed everywhere. But through the devastation, Random could make out a body at the top of the stairwell.

He picked himself up, just as he felt the floor give way underneath him. With a little run up, he vaulted the flamed in the doorway and made it into the hallway just as what was left of Anji's room plummeted to the ground floor. With little time to lose, he brushed the fallen beams that trapped Jason's unconscious body to one side.

Looking up, he noticed the roof was about to cave in too. With little room to escape, Random picked Jason up and rushed against the outer wall of the home, breaking through the bricks and mortar just as the roof burned into the top floor.

The pair landed in a heap amongst the rose bushes in the garden. Random checked that Jason was unharmed before witnessing the children's home collapse in a fireball.

He shook his head in horror and then noticed the sirens of the emergency services drawing ever closer.

Breaking out of the garden, he blinked his way past the flashing blue lights and spotted an ambulance close by.

'Oh Andrew, is he okay?' Miss Carter rushed over to him.

'Get a paramedic over here, quick!' screamed Jake as he and Anji also rushed to their friend's side.

'He's okay, no broken bones, just a bit of smoke inhalation,' Random reassured them as he handed the unconscious body over to the paramedics. Miss Carter stayed by his side as they rushed him into the ambulance, leaving the trio alone.

'Did you get everyone out?'

'Yes thankfully. Why would Sandman do that, Random? I don't understand. All those innocent children that could have been severely injured, or worse, killed.' Anji struggled to keep her shock in check. She shivered as the cold night air hit her.

'It was the Venus that caused that scene. Sandman must have rigged its laser cannon capability to draw me out.'

He looked ruefully at the rubble on the ground that used to be the care home. Fire crews were doing their best to put out the fireball but it was clear to everyone present that there was nothing they could do to save the building.

'He must be stopped,' said Jake, tears in his eyes, his face smudged with soot and snot.

'Come on then; we haven't got a moment to lose!'

Random tore away from the conversation and started running towards the school. With a big breath, Anji, closely followed by Jake, followed suit as the trio made for their final showdown. They had to get to the school before the Sandman harmed anyone else.

*

The Venus II sailed obliviously through the night sky. Undetected by radar, invisible to the naked eye, its first deed of the night was done. Skateboard piloted the ship the few miles towards the school which was the agreed rendezvous point where Random would meet his end.

Not knowing the destruction he had just

caused, the little AI kept a track of the heat signatures of Random and his two earthling friends on the scanner.
But a feeling started to emerge down in his CPU. A tiny shard of regret trickled in his system. Skateboard felt a twinge of uncertainty. Almost as if there was a light trying to break through the foggy darkness he felt within. He did his best to bury it but then it came back, slightly brighter this time. It was a feeling he hadn't felt in a while that was burrowing to the surface; Remorse.

He kept it hidden, away from his corrupted files, and remained focused on his task.

Like a hawk in the night sky, the Venus II sailed on among the blanket sky and continued to hunt its prey.

*

Random's legs burnt as they carried him further and further away from his two companions. With super human speed, he blitzed the pavement, dodged the onrushing traffic, crossed pedestrians with precision and hurtled like a purple blur towards the school.

The roar of the wind soared in his ears as he gained on the school and before long, what would have been a short bus journey for any normal human being, the school was in sight.

He totally forgot about Anji and Jake, who were well and truly eating his dust as they huffed and puffed their little legs along.

Random's entry to the school grounds was hindered by a big metal gate, with a sign adorning it's iron poles instructing that TRESPASSERS WILL BE PREOSECUTED. Random ignored the warning completely and shoulder barged his way through the gate, like a hammer through glass.

The gates shattered and splintered into tiny black toothpicks and the sheer force generated by Random's actions scattered the shards of metal into nearby trees and the concrete ground like javelins. But still, Random didn't care.

He came to a stop in the school playground. Panting and sweating, he scanned the area. The playground was calm and still. Random was unnerved. There was a haunting stillness as the shadows of the play equipment loomed against the few lamps that lit up patches of the vicinity.

A cool breeze blew through the swings and set Random on edge. He jumped and let out a sigh of relief when he saw that it was nothing.

'Come out then. I know you're out there so show yourself!'

Random's voice was hoarse from the fumes in the burning home. He could taste the black

smoke in his lungs. It burnt, but nothing was

going to stop him putting an end to the terror.

All of a sudden, his senses picked up on a trickling sound somewhere behind him. He turned to face the long jump sand pit.

'Of course,' said Random, clenching his fists tightly.

A tidal wave of sand grew in front of him, a full ten feet tall.

Random's mouth fell open, aghast at the vastness of the wall of sand that now stood before him.

Jake and Anji finally made it to the school.

'Anj…I…don't…think I can…'

Jake fell on the floor, his stomach rising and falling quicker than it had ever done before. Anji rested her arms on her knees, drinking in every gulp of air like it was lung nectar. She peered through the decimated gate and through the sweat that was dripping from her brow, she saw Random and what he was facing.

'Oh no!'

She tore off again, desperate to help her friend. 'Get up Jake! Random needs our help!'

Jake dragged himself up to his feet and saw the wall of sand.

Gulping, his legs tore off to help his friends, totally against the wishes of his brain, which told him to save himself and get away to safety as fast as he can. But then again, Jake knew better than to listen to himself and apart from the very odd exception, never did. And he wasn't about to start now.

'You think you can stop me, boy?' A demonic face began to form in the wall, grinning with murderous menace at his enemy.

'I don't think,' said Random. 'I know.'

'Let's see you try…'

The wave roared. It fizzed and pulsated. Before long, it started rippling and falling from its vertical stance and rushed with ferocity towards Random. The Rodasian stood, fists lifted to his face, ready to defend and most of all, attack.

Anji edged closer and closer to the playground but she watched on helplessly as the wave roared and with brute force, crashed over her friend. The sound of the wave crashing to the ground sent a shockwave that knocked Anji flying, its sheer ferocity like an explosion. The teenage girl opened her eyes and witnessed the sand sprays shoot upwards. Then there was a terrible calm… and Random's body was missing completely.

XV

Out of nowhere, laser bolts fizzed through the air towards Anji's shocked, motionless body.

'Anji! Down!'

Jake pulled her out of the firing line and they rolled down the grassy hill.

There was no time to talk or to catch their breath.

Anji pulled herself up to her feet and dashed for cover, with Jake not far behind. They took shelter under a small canopy that covered the entrance to the sixth form college. The Venus, still fully cloaked, opened fire on the brickwork obscuring the two teenagers. Jake and Anji tried ducking, protecting their ears from the terrible noise of the explosions surrounding them. They were not trapped, not just yet, but they had roughly thirty seconds before the entire sixth form college was nothing but rubble.

'Remember the plan!' shouted Jake. 'We need to get aboard the ship and get inside.'

'How?'

Jake searched his mind and found nothing.

Anji knew what to do. 'I've got it!' She edged away from the doorway and made for the gym shed, not two hundred yards away.

'Anj, what are you doing?'

The laser canons swung away from Jake's hiding place and targeted Anji instead.

'Noooo!' screamed Jake.

A trail of fire hammered into the ground behind Anji, knocking her off her stride but somehow she kept going. She ran closer and closer to the shed, the searing heat of the shots beginning to tickle the backs of her legs but Anji knew what she was doing.

The Venus fired one more shot. Anji dived out of its path just as the bolt exploded into the side of the shed, blowing broken wood everywhere. She shook herself off and raced into what was left of the shed, hoping the resources she needed had not been blown away too.

Luckily, the equipment wasn't too damaged and she grabbed for the goalkeeper nets. Was she going to attempt to catch the spaceship like a tadpole in a pond? She wasn't sure. To her relief, she found that a large stack of jump ropes had not been destroyed.

'Hey! Over here you stupid little machine!' Jake goaded. He sprang on his heels and started drawing the fire away from Anji. He trusted her implicitly…whatever she was planning!

Anji, loaded up with as much as she could carry, left through the hole made in the shed by the lasers and fixed her eyes on Jake. Now, to catch an invisible craft!

*

Random punched and punched at the sand that engulfed him. He held his breath and closed his eyes, refusing any bead of the Sandman that dared to enter his body, but he was losing the fight. He had to get to the surface.

Kicking as hard as he could, he fought to propel himself to the surface. But all the sand around him was dragging him lower and lower into the pit. He was being pulled closer and closer to a dry grave. Punching and kicking furiously, he seemed to make a breakthrough. The tidal wave groaned and heaved as a hole appeared in the space that Random had hit.

This was his chance.

With every ounce of strength, Random threw his body at the hole and jumped onto the high ground. Thinking on his feet, he sprang to his left and left the pit completely. He shook the grains of sand from his person and dug out the beads that threatened to trickle into his nose and ears with his index fingers.

'I knew you were incomplete,' panted Random. 'Give it up, Sandman. You can't drown me. Looks like you'll have to face me like a man instead!'

'Very well,' hummed the pit.

The sand shook and formed into the man that Random originally met back on Rodas.

'If you want a proper fight, I'll give you a proper fight.'

A fist shot six feet through the air and cracked against Random's jaw. The boy fell to the floor. He touched the affected area. It felt grazed and hot.

Random smiled.

'Finally.'

He sprang up and met the Sandman at eye level and launched himself, spittle falling from the corners of his mouth as he screamed. The rivals charged towards one another and met in a crescendo of fists and fury.

*

'This isn't you, you know.'

'Who said that?' said Skateboard.

'You did.'

'What do you mean, "you did"?'

'This is you, talking to yourself.'

Skateboard hummed. 'Go away, I'm busy.'

'What, shooting at children? That's not busy, that's a classic example of destructive behaviour.'

'No, it isn't.'

'Whatever it is, it certainly isn't a healthy way to go about your day.'

'Well, I'm occupied, whoever you are, and I'd appreciate a clear mind.'

Skateboard continued to fire the laser missiles at the blonde teenager below. The Venus was swinging like a bird of prey in the sky.

'Well, why do you keep missing?'

Skateboard was bemused.

'What?'

'If we are an AI with more skills, capabilities and resourcefulness than a sonic Swiss Army Knife, then why can't we hit him?'

'…I…'

'It's because you don't want to, that's why.'

'I do!'

'You really don't. That's also why you didn't kill anyone at the children's home either. It isn't in your programming to kill, no matter how corrupted it might be.'

Skateboard was starting to get angry.

'Look, I don't know where you have come from, or what the gleush you really are but could you kindly go away?'

'I was here first.'

'Vard off!'

Skateboard was going to have to be patient with himself.

'But I can't. I can't go anywhere. I'm you. I've always been you. I'm you more than you are right now.'

'That doesn't make a blind bit of sense.'

More laser fire shot out of the Venus' canons

and blasted a dozen fiery holes into the school. Fire and explosions spat out of what had, only moments before, been the school hall but was now a warzone.

'You've tried to bury me away but the Sandman didn't allow for another defect in your programming.'

'I don't have any defects in my programming!'

The voice inside Skateboard's mind began to gain a hold on the doubt corrupting his mainframe.

'Then how come I'm still here?'

Skateboard fell silent and stopped firing for a moment.

'Even artificial intelligence can have a sub-conscious that can lurk to the surface if it feels it's not following its core programming. We were created to help and serve. Not to seek and destroy.'

'But I'm fine.'

'You're not. Your files are corrupted. There's a bug in the system. Your files need a clean-up.'

The feelings of remorse that Skateboard had repressed earlier rose to the surface again. All of those terrible acts of violence; leaving innocent children now without a home, nearly taking a life…

'No! Don't. He'll kill me!'

'Don't worry, I'm working on it. There's no way that you'll short circuit with me here.'

'Stop it!'

Skateboard started to wrestle with his inner voice.

'Get out...of my head!'

'You need help, Skateboard. Let me get you that help.'

A switch automatically flipped from off to on.

Outside, the spaceship was now visible for all to see. Jake paused to allow himself a breath or two.

'No time, Jake, grab this!' Anji flung a skipping rope to him. Catching it in his sweaty palms, Jake stared at his friend in bemusement.

'Just swing it at the gantry!'

'But I can't tie knots!'

Anji rolled her eyes. Why, in a moment of crisis, did she need another reminder of just how bleeding ignorant Jake could be from time to time?

'Fine. Grab hold of me.'

Jake dropped the rope, just as an explosion ripped through the building behind him.

'There goes the science corridor,' he muttered. He slipped behind Anji and braced himself.

The pair watched as the flames licked higher around what was left of their school and as the Venus continued to hurtle uncontrollably in the air, edging closer and closer to the ground.

'There's no room for you in here!'

Skateboard flew himself around the cockpit, spinning and crashing repeatedly into the control panels and walls.

'I was here before you!' he screamed at himself.

The out of control AI noticed the fight occurring between Random and the Sandman, as both continued to pulverise one another with a flurry of fists and kicks. Then he spotted the pair of teenagers hovering just under the belly of the ship. Skateboard's sub-consciousness struggled to operate the outer door.

'No! I can't fail. I can't! We must destroy the boy. I have my orders.'

Skateboard's inner voice tutted, having gained an upper hand.

'Now I know you're broken. You forget, we don't follow orders. We have free will.'

The inner voice had won. For now.

The outer door creaked open, willing Anji and Jake inside.

'Now!' screamed Jake. Anji lassoed the skipping rope onto the gantry and hit it first time. What luck!

'Pull!'

The pair pulled their tired bodies up the rope. The Venus II hovered barely six feet from the ground but the climb inside the ship felt like a trip up Mount Snowdon using a cocktail stick as hiking support!

Anji had barely any strength left in her arms. Her limbs burned and rubbed against the plastic rope but inch by inch, she was getting closer.

With one final effort, she hauled herself inside. Panting as she lay on the cold metal floor, she failed to notice that Skateboard was awaiting her.

'Madam…I've relieved to see you.'

She jumped.

'Skateboard, you've been brainwashed. Please, don't hurt me.'

'Hurt you…no, Madam, I'd never do a thing like that.'

Anji was pensive.

'I don't want to hurt you…I want to kill you!'

A small gun protruded from Skateboard's body as he trained its sighters on the helpless girl.

'Hey Skateboard, suck on this!'

Jake, fully seizing his chance to be a hero, rolled into the mid-section and stuck the magnet Random gave to him to the chassis of the AI.

Skateboard began to spin uncontrollably. A scream emitted from his body and after a few seconds, the high pitched bawl turned to silence and Skateboard's body ceased spinning and came to a total stop.

Jake and Anji looked at each other in total silence.

'Well…I couldn't think of a better line!' said

Jake.

Anji threw her arms around him and gave him the biggest hug she had ever awarded to anyone.

Jake hugged her back and they shared a moment of tranquility after all of the elimination they had seen.

Anji pulled herself away.

'We're not done yet.' She went to Skateboard's side and noticed a pile of what looked like black soot that had emptied onto the floor by his side. Jake inspected further. The soot appeared more like black, glassy flecks.

'Is that what I think it is?'

'Burned sand?'

Jake pulled the magnet off Skateboard and noticed a blinking green light on his chassis.

'REBOOT.'

'Do you think it's safe?'

'It is now,' Jake pushed his finger against the light and Skateboard, the real Skateboard, no longer corrupted by the Sandman's poisonous mind, started flickering back to life.

Anji breathed a huge sigh of relief and looked out of the gantry door.

'It's up to Random now.'

XVI

The fight between aliens from a far-off world had moved quickly through the ruins of the school grounds. The Sandman's powerful jabs occasionally caught Random off guard, sending his sprawling with yet more flesh scuffed by the savage blows.

But Random was quick, much quicker than his impossible foe.

The Sandman shot another violent outburst towards Random's beaten face. Yet every new punch was becoming steadily weaker than the last. What's more, it left a trail of sand behind on the floor. Random had yet to notice both of these occurrences but his game plan was coming to fruition.

If his enemy continued to fight, he would soon be nothing but scattered particles of matter. And there'd be no power in the universe that could put him together again.

Random ducked and weaved his way through another barrage and continued to back away. His retreat had led him across the playground and towards the entrance of the school building itself.

Every now and then he hit back too but his attack was almost too powerful as he tore another hole through the Sandman's body. It didn't feel like he was making much connection with his opponent and every sucker punch almost ripped Random's own arm from its socket. No matter how angry he felt towards his attacker, it wasn't the thought of punching the Sandman to dust that was going to beat him.

It was becoming easier to pin point the parts of the villain's physique that was just borrowed from the sand pit as it was much darker and these particles were the first to drip away and fail to form back after one of Random's powerful upper cuts.

The Sandman was just as hard and fast as he had been at the start of their encounter. He rippled effortlessly towards the boy, cackling with every direct hit he landed on his person. As Random continued to back off, he was caught unaware by a crafty right-handed slice that cut the bottom of his left eye.

'All that genetic augmentation and I'm still a better fighter than you,' the Sandman hissed. 'What do you have in your locker now, boy?'

Random panted. He was determined to lull the Sandman into a false sense of security.

'You haven't won yet, Sandman,' he replied, wiping the purple blood away from one of the several cuts he had on his face.

The boy jumped head first into the man of

sand and burrowed his way through the being's torso. Spinning as he did so, he burst through the other side like a mole rising to the surface. He fell to the floor and grinned.

'Not the first time an alien has burst through someone's chest!' he chuckled, referencing a film that he had wished to see ever since his browse of the internet.

The Sandman stood aghast as he stared at the gaping hole in his body.

'It will take more than that to stop me!' A jet of sand shot from the Sandman's protruding hands and blasted Random clean across the playground. His trousers were cut to ribbons by the rough concrete as he travelled at great velocity before coming to a painful standstill at the foot of the entrance to the school building.

He smacked stomach first into the steps and coughed painfully. He tasted blood in his mouth and he ached in several different areas of his body. Struggling to get up, Random was aware of the fire that now raged throughout the ruined grounds. He stood with his back to the door and kept his eye on the Sandman as he bore down upon him.

'You're dead!'

'Gonna have to catch me first!'

In a flash, Random pushed his way ferociously past the locked doors and into the burning mayhem that used to be the foyer.

He was now a good several feet away from the Sandman, who screamed as another jet of sand bellowed towards Random. The boy was too quick and grabbed the beam, dropped on to one knee, twisted the Sandman to the floor and pulled him inside.

Whilst the Sandman recuperated from his fall, Random acted quickly. He sped up to the body of the Sandman and smashed it with both his fists, before disappearing further into the bowels of the fire.

The Sandman winced and spat a small amount of sand to the floor as if it were his blood. He tried to regain his composure but fell to his haunches almost immediately, more sand oozing from the areas of his body that felt like they had been punched to oblivion. If he were flesh and bone like he had once been, he would be a broken man by now. But he was not. He had nothing to lose. Laughing to himself, he sped off down the corridor after Random, dodging a flurry of sparks as he went.

Random held his breath. He had a fire extinguisher in his hand, ready to knock his predator even further into oblivion. He could barely hear the Sandman enter the corridor over the roar of the fires. The Venus really had done a number on the school, he thought. He'd have to remember to dismantle its laser canon capability when this was all over.

Hearing the trickle of sand grow ever closer, he readied the weapon. Raising it above his head, timing his attack ever so meticulously, he had misjudged it badly. The Sandman had somehow anticipated his attack and grabbed the other end of the extinguisher, yanking it from Random's grasp and smashing it at his chin, sending the boy soaring a couple of feet off the ground and hurtling to the floor yet again.

Random's jawbone broke instantly. He yelped as the searing hot pain flooded his fractured face. He nursed it with his hand but the agony was horrific. He had never broken a bone before. Now he knew just how terrible it felt!

The Sandman stood above him and raised the fire extinguisher high above his head.

'This is the end,' he spat.

Random tried to get up but he was too hurt by the last blow. This was it. He had failed.

'ARGH!'

The Sandman dropped the blunt instrument like a lead balloon and clasped his hands to his head.

Random scurried from underneath his enemy and crawled to the wall, clambering upwards to his feet.

'Skateboard...Skateboard!'

'Your connection's severed, Sandman,' Random said, his speech slurred. 'Looks like the human race has fought back. Well done Jake. Well done Anji.'

'This can't be!' the Sandman swayed from side to side, his head pounding like he had just awoken from a two-day party with the world's worst hangover.

'It's just you and me now. No puppets to help you, as it should be.'

Random felt a power surge shoot through his veins.

'Let's end this. Here. Now.'

He hurled himself at the Sandman, pushing him up the stairwell, delivering blow after blow as he went. The bulk of the fire seemed to have spread towards the top two floors. Random knew he was going to have to brave the flames and take his tormentor deep into the eye of the storm where the embers burnt hottest. There, he could put an end to the Sandman's misery for good.

The fighting continued. Inch by inch, Random took his foe closer and closer to the edge. The deeper they went into the school, the hotter the air became. And then something amazing happened. Random, betraying the fatigue he was feeling, threw a punch at the Sandman's left cheek.

CRACK!

Random looked down at his fist. Tiny clear flecks of beige crystals were imbedded in his knuckles. He looked up and saw that the part of the Sandman's jaw had turned to glass. He punched him again. Again, he recoiled as further shards collected in his hand.

'You're cracking up, Sandman. Give it up!'

The Sandman started to limp heavily. The components he had procured from outside his normal molecular imprint were betraying him. The sand was crystalising and soon there would be nothing left of him.

Another explosion ripped through the corridor, this time knocking both aliens over. A puff of sand signaled the Sandman's fall against the wall. The next thing that Random noticed was that the roof high above him was ablaze. There was absolutely no turning back. He was slap bang in the centre of the building and even with a run up, he'd find it difficult to get out without falling into the flames.

He looked over the stairwell. The whole hallway was awash with orange beacons of death. Not knowing where his friends were, he knew this was it.

Random glared at the Sandman, who was becoming nothing more than a giant glass impression of a melting person. Amazingly, he was still alive.

'All I wanted…' he struggled to talk as his facial features began to freeze, 'was to be complete again. You…will never know the horror of what I had become.'

'And killing me was going to get your old life back?' Random screamed loudly over the sound of the flames growing higher and higher. 'You became demented, twisted and evil. You killed to survive.'

'It's all I have known! All my life! Call yourself a Rodasian. From the cradle to the grave, we were bred for war!'

The Sandman tried to move but his feet were secured to the hot floor. He stared in terror as the sand that once made up his legs started to turn to hot, liquid glass. His torso began to subside.

'I was a man of honour! That's what they took from me. All Rodasian's had to pay!'

'Revenge solves nothing,' said Random. A beam fell between himself and his stricken foe.

'It was never going to get your old life back. It was never going to get your family back.'

The Sandman wept.

'I have failed them.' As the shadow of death began to envelop him, the Sandman thought of his wife and his children. That was his old life but maybe now his time was up, he would be with them again.

'Don't make their memory a sad one.'

Another explosion rippled through the hallway. Random fell to the floor, burning the palms of his hands as he held them out to protect his fall. The station holding one half of the hallway up had started to give way.

The Sandman, oblivious to the devastation he had caused all around him, wept uncontrollably. It wouldn't be long now.

A terrifying blast exploded from one end of the hallway.

Random and the Sandman looked on in horror as a fireball bigger than any either could ever dread to see started to tumble towards them.

The Sandman straightened himself up and with a stiffened arm and saluted Random.

'For Rodas?' said Random.

'For them,' replied the Sandman.

The fireball vomited into the hallway and in a matter of seconds the Sandman was gone, blasted into a million pieces, never to reassemble again.

Random took evasive action and narrowly missed being burnt alive by throwing himself to the ground and sliding down the hallway floor. Instantly, he knew that this was a bad idea as he was now hurtling head first towards a huge fire. He panicked and grabbed a hold of a broken grill, dangling perilously inches above the flames.

With great effort, he climbed back up the grill to his original position. Picking himself up, he assessed his situation. It was bleak. Coughing uncontrollably, he crouched as low as he could. He was going to perish. His clothes were starting to burn and stick to him. He was about to be barbequed.

The room was blacker than Kalor Meloso's heart. Random scrambled to grab hold of anything - SOMETHING - but he was giving in to the fumes. Now that there was no adrenaline to keep him going, Random knew he was toast.

He closed his eyes and decided that suffocation was a much more pleasant way to go than being burnt to cinder whilst still awake. Just like the Sandman before him, he accepted his fate.

The saviour of Rodas would be no more.

A mixture of images flickered in Random's mind as he succumbed to the fumes. People from his short life appeared before him once again,

although it wasn't Anji or Jake or Skateboard. It wasn't even his parents, who he had come to accept were the corpses he had discovered in that laboratory back on Rodas.

No.

It was the refugees.

He had failed to return to save them, like he had promised to himself. Oh sure, he was going to travel around a bit first, but he knew deep down that his sole meaning in the universe was to help them.

Random sighed, apologised to all of Rodas with a weak, 'sorry,' and lost consciousness.

*

'There he is, quick!'

Anji hollered over the sound of the Venus II's engines and the ferocious fires that engulfed what had once been St Thomas Secondary School. She clung onto the outer door of the ship but the intense heat made her cower inside again.

As soon as Skateboard had powered up again, the teenager had instructed him to scan for Random's body print. When they discovered that he was trapped in the burning school, they all feared the worst.

Despite his recent condition, the little robot acted quickly, imploring Jake to don a space suit from the munitions cupboard. After flying up to the very spot that Random was trapped in and seeing that his life signs were decreasing, Skateboard fixed a winch system to Jake's suit and gave him a spare oxygen mask to fit over Random as soon as he found him.

Anji kept a lookout on the scanner, checking

for Random's heat signature. She struggled to make him out in the smoke, such was the heat within the hallway, but upon finding him, she had rushed to the outer door where Jake was already making his descent. Cowering from the flames and choking from the fumes that were entering the ship, Anji watched through stinging, watery eyes for her two friends to appear again from the black smoke. She waited. And waited. And waited.

Seconds past like ice ages and still no sign of either Jake or Random. Until…

'Got him! Get us out of here quick!'

Skateboard instructed the Venus' mainframe to winch them up to safety. As they slowly ascended towards the ship, their clothes smoldering, Anji whooped in delight. Within moments, they were all safely aboard the ship again and Skateboard shut the outer door before bringing the ship through the fiery hole in the roof and sailing away into the starry sky just as the entire building crumpled in a huge fireball, explosions spitting into the night air.

Anji and Jake rested Random on one of the four medical bay beds. He looked atrocious; burned, bruised and broken. Anji made sure that the oxygen mask was fitted correctly and that he was still breathing. As they rested his body on the bed, an incubator-style cube descended from the ceiling and sealed Random in. Skateboard joined them in the medi-bay.

'Don't be alarmed, my friends. He is going to be alright. Sir's molecular structure is quite unlike anything else we've ever seen, I assure you. Give him a couple of hours in there and he'll be as good as new.'

Anji breathed a sigh of relief. It was over.

Jake yanked his helmet off his shoulders and emitted a long, deep gasp.

'Well…I'd like to say we had that covered.'

Anji shot him an all too familiar look.

'We nearly died!'

'Nah, not us. Not us lot.'

He walked over to a bench and plopped himself down.

'We're made of strong stuff, us lot. Skateboard, how are you feeling now?'

'My back-up disc is fully operational.'

'I'll take that as "okay" then, Anj?'

'What do you think? In the last three days we have discovered alien life, hidden it in our home, been terrorised by a man made of sand, had our home AND school burned to the ground and nearly been killed!'

'Well,' said Jake, scrambling for positives. 'What else were you going to do with your Monday night?'

Anji chuckled. 'Well, I never thought my pyromaniac days would come back to haunt me.' She looked into the middle distance. 'I mean, we burnt our school down.'

Jake patted her on the back.

'Yes. I know. Still. At least we don't have to think of an excuse if we wanted to pull a sicky tomorrow!'

XVII

Jason gazed up at what used to be his home. It had been a few days now since the fire, and while he was under, he had no idea of the other terrible act of vandalism that had occurred at St Thomas School. But when he came too, he was totally shell shocked. Blown away would be a good way to describe Jason's feelings but he wouldn't dream of saying that to any of his friends or colleagues for fear that it was too close to the knuckle.

He resisted the urge to climb under the police tape which had cornered the old place off. Jason wanted to burst into the building and see if any of his possessions had survived the blaze.

'Terrible, isn't it?'

Jason turned around to see Random standing behind him. He laughed.

'It was my first job. Well, in this industry, anyway. I was a barman first. And then, I don't know, I just wanted to help out. Make a contribution with my life.'

'I know how you feel,' agreed Random.

'This house stood for over a hundred years, y'know. It used to be a baker's. For decades a family run business operated from here, delivering bread and cakes to the locals. Now look at it.'

'Jason,' Random approached the care worker. 'I just wanted to say that I'm so sorry for what happened.'

'Did you know I'd be here?'

'Yes. Just call it a hunch.'

'Miss Carter?'

Random chortled. 'Got it in one.'

'I knew it.'

Jason walked up to face Random. He towered over the purple boy.

'Why are you apologising?'

'I...'

'Because you did it? You attacked us and the school?'

'Of course not.'

'Then why are you apologising? I don't like it when people do that for no apparent reason.'

'You could call it a guilty conscience, in a manner of speaking.'

A look of guilt past over Random's face.

'All that spiel you gave me about not being an alien. It was a lie, wasn't it?'

Random nodded.

'I've had this burning feeling in the back of my head ever since last weekend that something was not right. As soon as you turned up things started getting weird...tell me honestly. Were the people who did this after you?'

'Yes. Yes they were.'

'Look, what I'm about to say betrays my entire coda. Every caring fibre in my being, so I'm sorry if this sounds confrontational. But I don't know who you are or where you come from, "Andrew", but I think it is best that you don't keep in contact with the kids in my care ever again.'

'I understand,' said Random. He turned to leave.

'Wait,' Jason called out. 'Do you think they will ever come after us...or you...again?'

'No, you will never come to harm again. I can guarantee that.'

Random walked away.

'Hey, Andrew,' said Jason.

Random turned on his heel.

'Take care of yourself. Wherever you go.'

Random smiled, nodded his head in appreciation and walked out of Jason's life forever.

*

Sunshine fell through the thick woodland as Random walked with purpose through the forest. This whole area had been recommended by Anji as somewhere that the team could hide whilst they recovered from their bruises and bumps. It was Random who took slightly longer to recuperate, after all, he had enough smoke in his lungs to fund a cigarette company for a whole year and his broken jaw took a little time to reset. But the Venus had sorted him out. What a ship. He smiled as he thought of the tremendous craft. It was home…the only real home he knew.

He concentrated on the tracking device in his outstretched right hand. It bleeped intently all the way throughout his journey, on foot, through London and onto the outskirts of Essex.

He wanted to take the bus but on second thoughts decided that he might cause unwanted distraction again. So, a four-hour-long stroll it was instead. But on reflection, Random needed it.

The boy felt guilty; guilty for all the suffering his time on the Earth had caused. Thanks to him, the children would have to be re-homed. Classes upon classes of schoolchildren would also have to be relocated. Sure, those like Jake were ecstatic that their school had been reduced to nothing but smoldering rubble but the education of the many would be deeply affected.

Then there was the whole episode with the Sandman. Yes, he was evil, possessed by power and his own injustice but was it necessary for him to die? Was that what Random had to become to stop the evils of the universe that he had to face?

And what about those refugees back on

Rodas? It was they who occupied his mind in his moment of death, not his friends. He had a duty to protect them, to save them. But he still was not ready. Every passing second, more pain and suffering was happening back in that far flung part of space known as Ursa-17.

How could he stop it? Was it even at all possible?

Quietly, Random kicked the twigs and moss that lay in his path and solemnly came to the conclusion that he probably couldn't. But there was one thing he could control; his own ship.

The Venus II looked magnificent as Random entered the clearing. Its glimmering dark hull and seda metal shimmered and gleaned against the afternoon sun. Outside, three familiar faces awaited him on the gantry.

'You took your time, Sir. Everything okay?' enquired Skateboard.

'Yes, everything's fine. I just fancied a walk back.' Random smiled.

'How was Jason?' asked Anji.

'A bit shaken but he'll be alright. I did some snooping. Both fires have been blamed on local gang members, something about an orphan who used to belong to the same home as you two who had a grudge about his upbringing. It isn't watertight but it fits.'

'And the Sandman?' asked Jake.

'Gone forever. There's no way he could have survived the fire. He was far too unstable, both physically and mentally.'

Anji looked anxious. 'What about his other half back on Rodas?'

'No need to worry about that, Madam,' Skateboard helpfully chirped. 'When the Sandman's molecular imprint began to cease its function it would have had the same effect back on Rodas. He would have turned to ashes just as his form here on Earth did.'

'You mean sand?' corrected Jake.

'If you say so, Sir.'

'His body crystalised in the shear heat from the fire,' said Random.

'Ironic, isn't it'? said Jake. 'The Sandman was undone by what he used to destroy.'

'What do you mean, Jake?' asked Random.

'Y'know, fire.'

Random and Anji nodded thoughtfully.

'Or is that coincidence? I'm always getting those two mixed up.'

'It's irony, Jake,' laughed Anji.

'Is it? I can never tell,' said Jake wistfully.

'I know he was bad but considering what he had been through...' Random stepped up the small ramp and turned to face his two human friends.

'How are you two holding up?'

'Good, thanks,' smiled Anji.

Jake clapped his hands together.

'So…what now then, eh?'

Random looked at his ship.

'There's no way we can stay here. Skateboard and I don't belong here.'

Anji looked down, a hint of sadness in her tone, 'Then where will you go?'

'Anywhere,' grinned Random.

Jake had been holding onto his question for the last two days and could no longer contain it.

'Can we come?'

Random looked shocked.

'What?'

'Yeah. Can we come with you? I've always wanted to travel?'

'But…this planet is your home.'

'We can come back to it anytime,' said Anji. 'We know it'll always be here.'

'Will it now!' said Random, flummoxed. 'I don't know if I'll ever come back though. I'd be taking you away from your home.'

'Ah, correction,' Anji interrupted. 'We lost our home. We have nowhere to go.'

'But, Jason will be worried about you.'

'It doesn't matter. Please?'

Random sighed. 'I can't guarantee your safety. You've seen how dangerous it is.'

'Yes, but the Sandman's gone now, isn't he, and as far as you're aware, that Maloso fella is still trapped on Rodas, isn't he?' said Jake.

Random was running out of excuses.

'Skateboard, help me out here?'

The little robot shifted uncomfortably in his spot.

'Well…we could always do with some more company out in space.'

'Skateboard!' Random couldn't believe his ears!

'We want to see the wonders of the universe.

Just like you Random,' said Anji.

'Wouldn't you prefer to do that with friends than on your own?'

Random looked both his companions in the eye. They wanted to join him. More than anything they had ever wanted in their entire lives. Considering all three of them were orphaned, maybe there was something about kindred spirits, ready for adventure and excitement that bound them together.

'All right then,' Random conceded.

Jake and Anji cheered and hugged each other. Then the pair gave Random a group hug and even Skateboard received a warm embrace!

Anji kissed Random on the cheek and he blushed uncontrollably.

'Right, that's settled then,' said Random,

regaining a level of composure. 'Shall we be off?'

'Where shall we go first?' cried Jake.

'Anywhere in particular, guys?' asked Random.

'I don't know…' said Anji. 'Let's pick at Random.'

'Ugh. How cheesy was that!' chuckled Jake.

The trio smiled at each other and clambered inside the spaceship. After a couple of minutes, the roar of the ship's engines tore through the forest. The Venus II's hull blipped from sight as the cloaking device came into force.

As the friends took their positions in the cockpit, the Venus II launched clear of the woods and sailed off into space; away from Earth and away from home, but towards planets that all of them couldn't wait to explore.

EPILOGUE

The church door tore away at its hinges as the soldiers raced through. Shrouded in smoke, they broke their way into the holy sect; a quiet, modest place of worship on the corner of the street. The High Commander, regaled in all his crimson splendour, stepped through the door.

'Find her.'

A dozen or so soldiers searched the aisles. Every nook and cranny was explored but still no sign of her.

The soldier grew impatient, until suddenly, one of them looked up to the pulpit.

There, with a bucket in her hand, was a little girl.

The High Commander strode to the front and held his hand up to the child.

'Now, listen. Don't do anything foolish. We know what you have there. Just hand it over to us and we'll make sure no harm comes to you. Do you understand me?'

The little girl lifted the bucket over her head.

An air of panic started to emit throughout the church.

'Don't you dare.'

The High Commander began to sweat.

The little girl tipped the bucket.

'Take her out!' the High Commander ordered but it was too late. A sea of bright purple ooze started to flood down on the soldiers, coating their crimson suits in a colour only recently invented on Rodas, after centuries of trying.

The army ran out of the church in fright, shrieking like all their worst nightmares had come at once.

The little girl, alone now in the place of sanctuary, put the bucket down and smiled to herself.

She had plenty more where that came from. And it was keeping her family safe from the Crimson Empire and the Sapphire Regime.

She'd protect them. The boy who fled Rodas and disappeared amongst the stars told her it was possible when he escaped both the Crimson Empire and the Sapphire Regime.

All she needed to do was mix red and blue...

ACKNOWLEDGEMENTS

To Sophie - whose love and proofreading skills know no end.

Anthony Moorin for his fantastic artwork and for his patience.

To the family, as always.

The Diddly Dum boys, Doc, Mark and Allan

The adventures of Captain Random will continue
in *The Eater of Souls*.

Lightning Source UK Ltd.
Milton Keynes UK
UKHW01f0753110918
328671UK00006B/483/P